Amish for a Week

"May God guide us both, for eternity is so long..."

-An Amish friend from Kentucky

Ashley Emma

To my mom, Susan, who started all of this. Thanks for the books about the Amish…and thanks for everything.

To David, the love of my life, for encouraging me the most.

AMISH FOR A WEEK

Previously called Ashley's Amish Adventures

Copyright © 2020 by Ashley Emma

Other books by Ashley Emma on Amazon

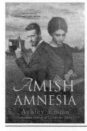

Coming soon:

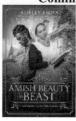

Praise for *Amish For a Week (previously called Ashley's Amish Adventures)*

"A refreshing glimpse inside Ashley Emma's writing process. Reading about her in-depth, genuine curiosity and appreciation for the people she met on her adventure into the Amish community felt like an intimate behind-the-scenes tour."

--Marie Schaeller, bestselling author of *Breaking the Chains of Silence*
http://www.Marieschaeller.com

*****

"Ashley Emma is a brilliant author. I admire her work. I was wondering what it is like to be Amish and also what it is like to be inside an Amish community. Through her books, she leads the readers into an unknown environment. She does it in a way that does not make me feel lost or left all by myself. She holds the reader's hand all along through the story. Therefore, I recommend you get a tour with Ashley Emma in her Amish world."

Ndeye Labadens, multi-bestselling author of *African Memories: Travels into the Interior of Africa, Secrets Book Launch Journey to the Ultimate Success, Relocation without Dislocation: Make New Friends and Keep the Old, and Australian Memories: Discover the Aussie Land and the Mysterious Red Center*

*****

"An intriguing and riveting read! This book gives readers a very rare peek into life in an Amish community. The author personally immersed herself into the Amish life, in order to authentically portray their passion for contentment, simplicity, and faith as the setting for an adventure of a lifetime. While it is an easy read, it is very intriguing and riveting! The author has a way of drawing a reader into every scene and keeping the momentum going. The characters she introduces us to are so real and relatable, despite the fact that they live such distinct lives from what would be considered main stream modern America! In fact, there is a sense of envy that causes an inevitable reflection on what we consider to be necessary and essential in our daily lives. It was a refreshing read!"

--Tracy Lee, author and pastor

*****

"An amazing read, and I thank the author for sharing her story and experience living with the Amish. It removes the mystery of the Amish, and how they live without the many amenities, we take for granted. There is much we could all learn from them and most certainly recommend reading this book."

-Marlene Wagner, author

"I LOVE these Amish books by Ashley Emma. They not only grab your interest and keep you reading, they give you a feel like you know a few Amish people and care about them. This is the most powerful step to understanding a culture different from your own. Thanks, Ashley, you have broadened my horizons and you made it fun on the way! There is also a homespun gentleness and honesty about the spiritual side of these differences. If everyone acted like this, Christianity would have a better world view and there would be less hatred in the world. There is nothing more we could ask for from a few books!"

--Chris McKay Pierce, author of *Customer Service can be Murder*

" It was interesting to me as I was able to learn more about the manner in which the Amish live. This one was about a wedding and that is something I had never read about previously. The wedding itself is 3

hours long but the actual vows and ceremony take about 5 minutes...
And, there is no finery at the wedding. This one also contains a visit to
Lancaster, PA. ...Highly recommended."

--USN Chief, Ret..VT Town, Amazon Top 500 Reviewer

Author's Note and Some Important Information:

This is a 100% true account of my time in the Amish community in Unity, Maine. All the people in this book are people I met during my stay there. All last names have respectfully been left out or changed. I did not embellish this story in any way. It is completely factual.

Please note that even though most of this book is written in past tense to make it easier to read, most of the information in this book is still current. Some present tense writing will be mixed in with past tense writing so it makes more sense.

These photos were taken over eight years ago, back when I had an old cell phone that did not have a good camera. I couldn't afford a good quality camera at the time.

I wrote this journal back when I was twenty years old, so the "voice" or writing style of this book may reflect that fact in this genuine, unique inside look into the Amish lifestyle. (However, the book has been thoroughly edited to improve the writing while still maintaining its voice.) Now, enjoy the experience as you join me on my Amish adventures.

Ashley Emma

Table of Contents

November 9th, 2011 – Going to Unity

A Note about the Amish:

When I was fourteen, I wrote a manuscript about traveling back in time because I imagined what it would be like, but I never thought I'd come close to experiencing something that incredible. But when I lived with the Amish, it was almost like traveling back in time.

To do research for my bestselling Amish novel, *Undercover Amish,* and my novel *Amish Alias*, I lived with three Amish families and have visited them several times over the past few years. This book is the product of all my research, adventures, and experiences I had while living in the Amish community of Unity, Maine.

I did not originally plan on writing a book about my research, but so many of my readers wanted to know what it was like for me to live in an Old Order Amish community, so I decided to write this documentary.

While I was in the Amish community of Unity, Maine to observe their culture, I did not stand on the sidelines. I dressed like them, got my hands dirty, and did everything they did. I wanted the entire Amish experience that Charlotte, the main character in *Amish Alias*, would have as she left everything she knew to take refuge and hide with her younger sister in an Old Order Amish community, afraid for their lives after traumatic experiences.

The Amish are a truly amazing, kind, and smart group of people, as you will discover in this book. The Amish church began hundreds of years ago, but the Amish today are not very different from the church founders.

The only things many people know (or think they know) about the

Amish are what they have learned from TV, movies, or Amish romance novels. These can sometimes stereotype or falsely portray the Amish. In fact, my Amish friends in Unity choose not to read Amish love stories for this reason. Hopefully this work will help break some of these stereotypes.

In the Bible, God calls his followers to live "separate" from the world. Many Christians think that means merely not doing some things other people do, but the Amish take it literally. In fact, they take many of the things in the Bible literally. The Amish do indeed live separate from the world—not only by their location, but in the way they dress, pray, travel—in virtually every aspect of their lives.

I think the Amish understand and know just as much or even more about the world than *Englishers*, or people who are not Amish. The Amish are hard workers, and family and friendship are so much more important to them than material objects. They do not need possessions to be happy, and believe me, they are happy. I highly respect them.

Growing up, I suppose I knew the Amish dressed in old-fashioned garments, but I didn't know anything else about them. Then about a year ago, my mother gave me some Amish novels. I read several of them. (Later I would learn many of the books I read are banned by Amish parents.) I became completely fascinated with the ways of the Amish. I just wanted to learn more about them.

In case you don't know much about the Amish, here is some basic information. The Amish (not to be confused with Mennonites) live very simple lives. They believe being content with a simple life is important because God looks at the heart, and God needs to be first in one's life—not possessions. That is why they do not need material things to be happy.

There are the Old Order Amish, who live without electricity and vehicles, and there are the New Order Amish, who may own vehicles or use electricity. Each Amish community varies and has different ways and rules.

I wrote my Amish novels based on what I learned about the Old Order Amish community I stayed with in Unity, Maine. I wrote this book from my own observations and experiences with the people I lived with and met there. Much of this book was written in a notebook or on my phone as I lived in Unity. The laptop I owned at the time was a hunk of junk with a very short battery life.

All the characters in my Amish novels are based on wonderful Amish individuals I got to know in Unity. However, though their first names were not changed, all last names have been changed to respect their privacy, even though they did not ask me to do this. They know I write about them. In fact, they read my work and readily approve of it. They were happy to meet a writer who wanted to accurately portray them. Several of the characters in my novels are based on my Amish friends.

Even though I started going to Unity solely to do research for *Amish Alias,* my friendship with the Amish blossomed. I hope to return again soon.

I hope you enjoy this book and love learning about the Amish as much as I did and still do. For more Amish reading, check out my new bestselling novel, *Undercover Amish.*

-Ashley Emma

Sunday, February 5th, 2011

Today I had an idea. I decided to live with the Amish for a while.

I don't want to join the Amish. I just want to research a novel I am going to write. I need to go to a place where I can get away from worldly distractions and learn as much as I can.

I know very little about the Amish. Most of my knowledge comes from fiction-based media, and much of it could be wrong. Immersing myself in their culture will be a crash course in who they are and what they are about. I need to be thrown out of my comfort zone and learn to live without everything I'm used to—electricity, chaos, and shortcuts. I want to know what it's like to leave everything familiar and have to live with a family I don't know in an Amish community. That is going to happen to the main character in *Amish Alias*, and I want to portray her situation accurately.

I have no idea how I will be able to write when I am there, though. I want to bring my laptop, but it is old and the battery dies so quickly, and I don't know where I will be able to plug it in. I guess I will have to write everything in my notebook or on my phone, if I can find somewhere to charge it, and transfer my writing to my laptop later. I've done it before. My phone battery lasts a lot longer than my laptop battery, and it charges faster.

Wednesday, February 23rd, 2011

Last week I made several phone calls to inquire about living with an Amish family. Since I knew there are plenty of Amish in Pennsylvania, I called Lancaster County first. It would be a long drive for me, but I figured that was the closest Amish community, so I would just have to make the trip.

As the phone rang, I began to have doubts. Would they turn me down? Would my request offend them? Had anyone done this before? If so, how many? Maybe this was a common request after all.

Then someone answered the phone, disrupting my thoughts.

"Hello. I am calling because I would like to live with an Amish family for a short time. I am writing an Amish fiction novel, and I want to accurately depict the Amish lifestyle. I thought the best way to do so was to research a community first-hand and then use my own experiences as a reference. Are there any Amish families who would be willing to take me in for a little while?" My stomach fluttered with nervousness. I was not sure if they would be all right with me writing about them.

"There are several tours where you can come see the Amish community." The man's response was monotone, disinterested. "Many people come here to see the Amish."

"No, I don't want to be a tourist. I want to actually live with them. I want to live like them. I'd work with them, dress like them, and do everything they do. I need to immerse myself in the culture."

"Oh." He sounded much more interested in the conversation. "Are you thinking of joining the Amish?"

Okay, so he hadn't been listening to what I said. He probably fielded a lot of questions about the Amish lifestyle during the day, so I couldn't fault him for that. "No, no. I am really just doing research for a book I'm writing."

There was a slight pause. "Oh. I see this is a Maine number. Do you know there is an Amish community in Maine, in the town of Smyrna?"

"There are Amish communities in Maine? I didn't know that!" Maybe I wouldn't have to travel very far after all.

The man gave me the number to Smyrna. When I called, the man who answered told me about the Amish community in Unity, Maine, which is much closer to where I live. Unity is only two-and-a-half hours away from my house.

He gave me the number to Unity, and I placed my third call. The Amish in Unity do not have phones in their houses, but they do have phones in their businesses. I was given the number to a store, but no one answered. I left a message and awaited a reply.

A few days later, the owner of the store, an Amish man named Caleb, called me back.

"We would love to have you stay at our house. We have seven daughters and one son. The youngest is two, and the oldest is eighteen. We have plenty of room here," Caleb told me.

"Wow! Thank you! Do you mind if my mother comes with me?" Even though the Amish are commonly known as a gentle people, and because it is always safer to travel in pairs, I decided to bring my mom with me. I didn't want to travel alone my first time going, and she was more than excited to go. There was no one I would rather take with me, since she was the one who first got me interested in the Amish.

"No, of course not. She is welcome to. We are looking forward to meeting you both."

True, a family of eight children is rather large, but I love big families. "I'm from a big family too. I'm one of six children."

"Well, you will enjoy it here, then. Could you come this upcoming Saturday night into Sunday so you could come to church and meet the community?"

"That sounds great!"

Throughout our pleasant phone conversation, I didn't mention I was writing a book about the Amish. I wasn't sure what they would say if I told them. I wasn't trying to be deceitful. I just didn't want them to assume things about me until they met me first. I would wait until I got there and see how it would go.

When I asked Caleb on the phone what we should wear, he said we could wear anything we wanted as long as it was modest and conservative.

"What do the women there wear?" I asked him.

"They wear long dresses and head coverings. We would appreciate it if you dressed modestly, but we do not expect you to cover your hair."

I wanted to blend in with dresses of our own that were similar to the style of Amish woman's clothing. Later that day my mother, Susie, and I realized we had nothing old-fashioned enough to wear, so we went to Goodwill and got long-sleeved, floor-length dresses so we wouldn't stand out too much.

I've heard Amish church services are held in people's homes, are about three hours long, and are spoken in German. I've also heard that the Amish mostly speak Pennsylvania Dutch, a form of German, with their families when they are home. I took German for three years in high

7

school, but since then I've forgotten most of it. However, once I start studying it again, it always comes back to me quickly. I need to start reviewing it.

I got some books at the library today and did some research online about the Amish. I want to know as much as I can about their rules, customs, and lifestyle before I go so I can blend in.

I just can't wait to go to Unity! I hope this experience will really change me for the better and that I learn as much information for my novel as I possibly can.

February 27th, 2011

I am thinking of so many questions about the Amish. Will they mind if I write down the events of the day in my journal? Will they be all right with me going there to learn about their ways so I can write a book about them? Will they let me use their names for characters in the book? Would an Amish man be offended if I shook his hand?

What if I fall asleep during one of their three-hour church services and fall off my chair onto the floor? Someone has done that before in my church. What if I do something they consider offensive? Will they care if I use my cell phone? What if it rings at the dinner table?

What if I make one of the teens want to leave the Amish by telling them about the outside world?

What if?

I'm not scared. I'm just getting a little anxious.

I've told some people about my upcoming trip, and sometimes they say how they have visited the Amish country too, usually in places like Lancaster County, which is where everyone thinks I'm going. Many people like to visit to see the plainly dressed people and try to take pictures of them while they go on tours.

"Oh, yes, I visited Lancaster County during our vacation last year with my family, and we stayed in a hotel right outside the Amish community," one woman told me. "It was lovely there."

"No, I am not just visiting or going on vacation. I am going to live with them to do research for a book I am writing. I'm going to dress like them, work with them, and be like one of them for a week," I told her.

"Oh…wow," she said, eyes wide. "That's different. I've never heard of anyone doing such a thing. The Amish will actually let you live with them for a week, even though they don't know you? Do they know you are going to write about them?"

"I haven't told them yet. If they don't want me to write about them in particular, I will just not use their real names. And yes, they're fine with me living with them. It's amazing how trusting they are, actually. I'm not so sure I would let a stranger live with me and my family like that."

Some people tell me that going to live with people I don't know is dangerous. They think it's a scam, and that someone who is not actually Amish called me back and invited me to their house. Some think it's just plain weird, like I expected. Others are saying it's a good thing for me to do. I knew people would think many different things, but I have faith this will work out wonderfully.

I've decided that even though I am going to Unity to research my Amish novels, *Undercover Amish* and *Amish Alias*. While I am there, I will journal everything I do and make that into a documentary. I will call this journal *Ashley's Amish Adventure*. (Since then I have changed the name.) I have started to tell people this, and one thing is for sure—several people cannot wait to read all about it.

March 5th, 2011

I made Mom and myself some bonnet–like head coverings out of white handkerchiefs and ribbon ties today, just in case they ask us to cover our hair. We want to blend in with the Amish as much as we can, but I doubt they will ask us to wear head coverings. They probably won't expect us to do everything like them, but I want to try to make an effort, not just as a courtesy, but because it will help with my research.

The next morning, I put on my brown dress with some plain black boots that we got at Goodwill. Mom wore a green dress that had a pattern on it, and though the Amish do not wear patterns, it was the best we could find.

We packed up the car and left the house with a GPS and a plentiful supply of crackers and yogurt.

Mom had a thought that made me worry. "What if they laugh at us for trying to look like them?"

I hadn't thought of that! My stomach flopped.

About halfway through our drive, we stopped at a gas station for a bathroom break. I started to get out of the car when I realized how I was dressed. I almost didn't go in, but then I put on my long coat and decided to just do it.

A man stopped us at the door. *Oh no, he's going to ask us why we're dressed funny or make fun of us.*

"Sebago Lake!" he exclaimed, reading something on my mom's car. "I won a fishing derby there once!"

Relief washed over me. Maybe he didn't think we were strange at all. Is this how all Amish feel when they leave their community?

Do they do that often? Maybe they don't. And maybe they don't care what people think, anyway. I have a feeling they're secure in who they are. That's probably a refreshing way to live, being unconcerned about the latest fashions and newest releases. It's probably both liberating and grounding.

Or maybe I'm just reading too much into this, and the Amish have the same concerns and feelings we all do.

My stomach churned. There were so many intricate facets to this journey that I hadn't even considered. I had wanted to learn about their culture and way of life, but I hadn't even considered their feelings about it until walking in their shoes. Or dress, as it were. Blending in while learning was already proving emotionally difficult, even though so far it hadn't posed any real problems.

We finished at the gas station and got back on the road. On the way, we got a call from Caleb saying he was leaving his store for about an hour, and he wanted us to wait for him there until he got back. He said his assistant Louis would take care of us until his return.

My mother and I speculated about whether he had a car or if he was taking a horse and buggy. We really had no idea what to expect. I had read that most Amish did not own cars, but I had heard that some New Order do.

To pass the time while we drove, we called a relative to tell her about what we were doing.

She was shocked. "I wouldn't go live with a strange family in this day and age. They could be dangerous. You never know. What if they aren't even Amish and they murder you?"

We tried to explain that I'd done my research and due diligence. I knew they actually were Amish, and I knew how non-violent the Amish are. We would be completely safe with them. In fact, they are probably some of the safest, gentlest people in the world. I read in an article that there had never been an Amish murderer until the early nineties.

I then realized how surprising it was that Caleb didn't ask me questions like why I wanted to live with them or if I was a Christian. How extraordinary. He trusted God enough to let two strangers into his home and be around his children—without question.

They must have had incredible faith to let strangers into their home.

During the last few miles of our drive to Unity, I excitedly watched for signs of Amish life. So far, everything looked like any other small town. There were run-down gas stations, houses with cars in the driveway, and pizza restaurants. No buggies in sight. Were we in the right place?

We took a turn down a long road. The GPS said we only had a few more miles to go. I started to wonder if we typed in the right address. This looked nothing like what I had expected. Where were the black and white houses and the horses and buggies? Where were the men with beards and hats, and where were the women in long dresses?

I watched for houses with no shutters, no power lines, and no cars outside. I knew Amish houses usually don't have shutters, but they do sometimes have brightly colored curtains in the window.

Though some houses did not have shutters, almost all the houses we passed had cars in the driveway. I started to think the Amish here were New Order and owned vehicles. Had I made a mistake in coming here? I wondered how much information I could use to write my book from

Amish who used electricity and cars. That was not really what I wanted for my book. People wanted to read about the Old Order Amish because that lifestyle was so foreign to them.

Just when disappointment settled in, I saw a yellow street sign with a horse and buggy on it.

"Approaching destination," announced the GPS. "Your destination is on the left."

So we were in the right place. The disappointment I'd felt lifted, and a smile crossed my face. This was what I wanted.

To the left of us was a gray house with white shutters. I had always thought Amish houses were black and white. That's what I had seen in movies. Already I learned something, and we hadn't even reached our destination yet.

We found Caleb's community store at the next driveway over and pulled in. "Is this it?" I wondered out loud.

The store resembled a log cabin. It had a metal roof, and there was a large assortment of wooden furniture and bird feeders on the porch. Behind the store were two houses surrounded by wide fields with horses.

I looked around, got out, and followed Mom into the store. A friendly black and brown dog greeted us on the porch. We entered the store and the first thing I noticed was that it was so…eerily quiet.

(Below is a photo of the store taken from down the street.)

(Caleb's house is pictured below and part of the store's porch is on the right of the photo.)

No music played. There were only two other customers in the store.

I never noticed before how much music makes a difference in a public place. I guess I'd grown so used to excess background noise from TV and radio that I usually didn't notice music in stores.

But I noticed its absence in this one.

We approached the young man at the counter, whom Caleb had said would help us. The young man, Louis, said he knew I was coming once I told him my name. Caleb had told him about me.

"How long have you been talking to Caleb?" Louis asked.

I wondered why he asked, but didn't question him. "A few times on the store phone over the last few weeks."

"It's not the store phone," he said. "It's a phone the community shares. Anyway, did Caleb tell you he had a new baby girl a week ago?"

(Below is a photo of the phone shanty the community shares.)

(Below is a photo of some watermelons near the shanty that the Amish grew.)

"No," I answered. "How many children does that make?"

"Nine," Louis answered. "He has eight girls and a boy."

"And I thought six was a lot!" exclaimed my mom.

People always tell us that six children is a lot. To us, it's just family. I couldn't imagine it any other way. I looked forward to meeting Caleb's family. It would be nice to be with a large family again.

We asked Louis a long string of questions, starting with whether church was tomorrow.

"Church is every other week, and Sunday School is on the weeks that church is not on. Tomorrow there will be Sunday School, which is like church for everyone, but the service will be from 9 a.m. to 11:30 a.m. There would be a lunch after, and you are certainly welcome to stay. Everyone brings food to share."

He also said the service would be held in English, to our relief, and that church services are usually about three hours long.

Three hours?! Wow. I willingly go to church almost every week, but our services are only about an hour and a half long. At least this Amish service would be in English. I was actually excited to go to church to see what it was like.

I realized Louis was wearing clothes that did not look Amish. He had on a black zip-up vest and a shirt with buttons on it. I thought the Amish did not wear buttons. I had read that in a book.

Maybe he was not Amish. I asked him if he was, and he said yes.

Oh no, they wear clothes that aren't old-fashioned. I hurried out of the store and went inside the car. Mom followed.

"These are the only clothes we brought. They wear modern clothes! We are going to look so stupid!" I said.

Then Mom began to laugh.

"It's not funny!" I wondered what we should do, and even briefly considered driving back to the nearest town and buying some clothes.

Before I made a decision, I remembered I told my best friend, Kate, I would call her when we arrived. I called, but she didn't answer, so I left a message.

"Hi, Kate. We are here, and we are wearing long dresses and they wear modern-looking clothes. My mom won't stop laughing because we didn't bring clothes that we usually wear. They are going to laugh at us!"

My mom laughed even harder.

Just then, a pony wagon rolled by with a few women on it. They wore long dresses, somewhat like ours, along with head coverings!

"Oh, never mind!" I said, still recording a voicemail message. "We just saw a bunch of ladies go by, and we'll fit right in. Sort of."

I hung up, and we went inside the store again.

"Are we dressed appropriately?" my mom forwardly asked Louis.

He chuckled. "You will be fine," he said. "We understand you are not Amish, so you can even wear your regular clothes and we wouldn't mind, but with those clothes you will blend in."

I sighed in relief.

"So, is that Caleb's house over there?" I asked Louis, gesturing toward the gray house next door that we had seen earlier.

"No, Caleb's house is that way, behind the store." He spoke while organizing some things on the counter.

I went to the closest window and looked out. It was set far back into a field, on the edge of the woods, and had a very long, unpaved driveway. The house was tan and had a maroon metal roof. There were no shutters, and of course no power lines. There was a large, tall metal pipe coming out of the roof, like a chimney. It was a very nice, large house. And I had been expecting a small black and white house with an outhouse.

Just as we started talking to Louis again, my phone rang. I wondered if he thought that was rude.

I knew it was Kate calling, so I went outside to talk to her.

"I just got your message. It was hilarious!" she exclaimed.

I told her about the store and how we had asked Louis several questions, and I described Caleb's house. Then I went back inside the store, and my mother and I sat down in handmade rocking chairs from Lancaster County, Pennsylvania. I looked at a bookshelf next to us and read the titles. One of the books was the German *Ausbund*, or songbook, and I looked through it to see if I could understand any of it, but I only understood a few words. I tried to teach some German to my mom. She speaks French fluently, since my family is French (despite the family connection, I speak next to none), but she doesn't know any German.

It didn't matter, though. We would get by while we were here.

A little later, a man came into the store with a teenage girl who wore a long dress and prayer *kapp,* or white head covering that resembles a bonnet. They walked toward us, smiling.

This had to be him. "Are you Caleb?" I asked him.

"Yes, I am. It is nice to meet you, Ashley." He shook my hand then introduced us to the girl, his daughter Beth, who was fifteen. I introduced my mom to them.

"Sorry about the wait," he said. "We had to finish installing the toilet in the building where we will be having church tomorrow."

Oh, good. They had indoor toilets!

"It's okay. We kept ourselves busy and asked Louis a lot of questions. He was very patient with us," my mom said and smiled at him.

"Good. All right, let's go up to the house." He thanked Louis for welcoming us.

Below is Caleb's house and his barn is on the left.

(As you can see in the photo below, there is a lot of laundry that is done every week at Caleb's house!)

(Below are some photos of the fields near Caleb's house.)

(The house in the photo below is Caleb's mother's house.)

As we walked outside, my mom offered Caleb and Beth a ride in her car, but they said they would rather walk. So we got in the car and attempted to drive up the driveway, which was extremely slippery. Our car barely made it up. I didn't know how Caleb and Beth walked the whole way without falling.

(Below is a photo of Caleb's barn, some buggies and an old-fashioned Maytag washer.)

An adorable little girl in a prayer *kapp* watched from the house's front window as we approached. We parked, grabbed our bags, and went inside the house. It had taken us so long that we pulled in right after Caleb and Beth reached the house.

When we walked through the door, the first thing I saw were three dark-haired girls in pale blue and gray dresses sitting on a couch beside Caleb's wife, who was holding the newborn baby.

They told us to put our bags by the door, and we put our coats on the sewing machine. I expected white walls and drab décor, but was pleasantly surprised. The room's walls had been painted light blue, and the kitchen's walls were light yellow. To our left was a huge quilt in progress being held up on a wooden contraption that resembled a table with the quilt as the table top. In the corner near the quilt was some sort of nonelectric sewing machine. There was a door leading to what looked like a play room with stuffed animals on a bench. To the right of that was a bookcase with encyclopedias and well-known board games. Straight ahead of me was the couch, which had a blue pattern on it but was covered with a white sheet. There was no clutter. The walls were bare except for a clock and a calendar. There were no pictures, and it was all very clean and organized.

To our right was a long, plastic-topped kitchen table. I could hear chopping sounds and pots and pans clanging. Caleb's daughters bustled around, already making dinner. From where I stood, I could see the back of the gas stove, and I could feel its heat. One of the girls took a lighter from Caleb and lit the gas light above the table, which also gave off heat and surprisingly bright light. One of the other girls brought us chairs that were on wheels but had been covered with plain gray fabric.

We sat down, and all the children were introduced to us. Regina, who is eighteen, is the oldest. Then there is Cara, Beth, Elsie, Rosaline, Mary Esther, Joanna, two-year-old Jonas, and baby Emma Sue. Their mother's name was Rosie.

I realized that even though there were so many children in the house, it was very quiet besides the sounds of the girls cooking. There was no TV or radio, of course.

My house, which houses only five people, always has much more commotion than this house with twice as many people.

The girls went back to making dinner while the younger ones quietly read and my mother, Caleb, Rosie, and I talked. Mom and I told them about our family and how we homeschooled. I had gone to Veritas Academy for high school, which only had eight people in it at the time.

Then they asked us what we did for a living. "I'm a cosmetologist," I told them. My mother and I owned a salon together in our home at the time.

"What is that?" Rosie asked, confused.

"Mostly I go to elderly ladies' homes and wash their hair for them if they are unable to. And I cut men's hair," I said, and that was the majority of my job at the time. Since Amish women do not cut their hair, I left out that I do many women's haircuts. I also left out everything else, like hair coloring and highlighting and manicures and pedicures. I wasn't even sure if they would know what those things were.

"So," Caleb asked. "Why are you here? What do you hope to gain out of this experience?"

"I am fascinated with the way the Amish live," I said. "My mom gave me some books to read about a year ago, and ever since then I have wanted to learn more about it."

"There was something about writing a book," Caleb said. So, he had talked to the man I had called in Smyrna. There was no avoiding it. I had to tell him about my book.

"Yes, that's me. I write novels. I want to write a novel about a girl from the city whose parents die, and she has to live with her Amish family she never knew she had." I told them a bit more about *Amish Alias* storyline.

"See, usually Amish novels don't portray us correctly." Rosie shifted the baby in her arms. "I don't let my daughters read them. They are always about romance." I didn't understand what she meant at the time, but later on I would learn more about the process of Amish dating. Rosie continued, "It is not secretive or scandalous, like in many Amish romance novels. Amish dating is serious, with no physical contact whatsoever, and usually leads to marriage."

"I write Christian novels," I said. "That is why I am here. I want to learn as much as I can about the Amish so I can write my book correctly. I want to get everything right."

"My father was a writer," Caleb said. "He wrote a book called *Give Me This Mountain*. I am glad you have come to research before writing. Usually, as Rosie said, writers do not portray us correctly, but it is wonderful that you have chosen to."

I smiled, relieved. "So, are you all right with me writing about you and your family here? I can change your names, if you want."

"I am fine with that. You don't even have to change our names. I am just happy you have chosen to do this, to write about how we really are," Caleb said, surprising me.

I grinned. Joy bubbled up inside me. I could hardly believe they were fine with me writing about them.

After we talked for a while, Rosie told us we could bring our bags upstairs and see the rest of the house. Regina led us up to the second floor and showed us our room first. It had blue walls, a queen bed, a chest by the window, and a nightstand with a kerosene lamp on it. There was also a closet with spare dresses in it.

(Below is the view from out of the window. You can see part of Caleb's barn on the right.)

Then there was the bathroom. We were happy to see a toilet and a shower, but the sink had not been installed yet. They had been renovating the bathroom recently.

Regina showed us the rest of the girls' rooms. I was surprised to see mirrors and perfume and lotion in their rooms. What was the difference between those things and makeup, which wasn't allowed? My guess was that makeup alters the appearance and lotions and perfumes do not, but I didn't have the courage to ask. I didn't want to sound like I was criticizing their choices. Maybe once I knew them better…

We went back downstairs, and I offered to help with dinner.

"It's all right," Cara said. "You are the guest."

"I want to help. There has to be something I can do." I looked around the busy kitchen full of old-fashioned-looking girls. I had to blink a few times and remember I was still in the twenty-first century.

"We're making egg salad for church tomorrow," Regina said. "If you really want to help, you could peel the eggs."

"Sure!" That was something I knew how to do without electricity. Once I had them all peeled, rinsed, and mashed up for the egg salad, I asked what else was left.

"We just have to mash the potatoes, but I can do it," Regina said.

"I really don't mind doing it," I told her. "I do it at home."

"How do you usually mash potatoes?" Regina asked.

"By hand, with a masher." I wondered if there was some sort of electric potato masher sold in stores. We sure don't have one at my house.

Regina gave me the pot of potatoes. I usually do it the same way they do, except they add cream cheese to theirs, which made them really good.

I knew I'd be making mine like that from then on.

Soon dinner was ready, and we set the table. They used plastic dishes that were a cross between bowls and plates. We all sat down, and I realized I forgot to tell my mom they pray silently before dinner. At our house, we usually pray aloud. I hoped she wouldn't be too confused, and she wasn't. She said nothing and went along with it.

After the prayer, we passed the delicious food around the table. The girls made the mashed potatoes, gravy with meat in it, a green bean casserole, and corn. We also ate bread my mom brought with some jelly. I have to say, Rosie's help wasn't necessary with meal preparation. Those girls were great cooks!

They had started making dinner around 4:00 p.m., when we got there, and we finished cleaning up around 7:00 p.m. Dinner was a three-hour event—all without television or music playing in the background or cellphones going off. It was a much slower pace than meals I'm used to, but the food was so good, and we shared some great conversation. It was a pleasant change for me.

After we finished eating, they sang "God Our Father." Mom and I didn't know it, so we just listened, and it was so beautiful. Even the little children sang every word.

Afterward, I helped the girls wash the dishes.

"What do you like to do at home for fun?" Cara asked while she dried a cup.

"I like to draw. Do you draw?"

"Yes, we like to draw."

"What do you draw? Can you draw people?" I asked.

"Yes. I like to draw landscapes and animals though," said Cara. I was surprised they were allowed to draw people, since photographs are not allowed. I wanted to ask the difference, but the kitchen bustled with activity as we all tried to clean up, and the conversation moved on before I got the chance.

After we finished the dishes, Cara asked me if I would read to her younger siblings.

The younger Amish children do not speak much English. They speak only Pennsylvania Dutch until they go to school, and that is when they start to speak English.

While I read to them, I made funny voices for the characters, and I tried to be animated, so they smiled, even if they might have not completely understood what I was saying. As I was reading, I realized how strange it was to see the girls walking around in their long dresses and *kapps*, which I had only seen before on movies or the covers of books or in Amish movies.

Even though their lifestyle is different, we still have a lot in common. We all share many of the same interests and beliefs. If not for the old-fashioned clothes, I would have thought they were any other non-Amish Christian family.

After reading, I learned there was a Singing the next day at 6:00 p.m., but we heard it was supposed to snow at 12:00 p.m.

A Singing is when the community gathers to sing for a few hours, and sometimes Amish boys will give rides home to the girls they like. It is kind of like their way of going on a date.

It all sounded like fun, and I hoped we could go, but the threat of bad weather loomed in my mind.

Mom asked Rosie if there would be coffee in the morning, and Rosie said they made coffee regularly. Mom was very happy about that. She had been wondering whether or not she would get her morning coffee.

We all discussed how we would travel to church in the morning. My mom offered rides in her car, and Caleb said he would let his girls ride in it if they wanted to. He said it is not a sin for us to own a car because we are not Amish, but they believe it is better to own buggies because, for them, it's all about being content with what you have or can make. Though they did not own cars themselves, riding in someone else's car was permitted.

Around 8:00 p.m., we were sent to bed. Caleb gave us a battery-operated stand-up light that resembled a lantern. (See photo below.)

I was not used to going to bed so early. I don't recall sleeping at all that night. When I heard sounds of feet in the hallway and doors opening and shutting at 6:00 a.m., I was already awake and anxious to get on with the day. I jumped out of bed to get ready for church.

(Below is a photo of the view from our window which I took from my car.)

Afterward, I brought all our bags downstairs and put them in the car because Mom said she was pretty sure we would have to leave right after church before the storm hit. By the time I was done, the girls were done making breakfast. They made toast from the bread Mom had brought on a pan on the wood stove. There was fruit and store-bought cereal, too, in clear plastic containers instead of cereal boxes.

This time before we ate, Caleb prayed aloud, and we sang after we finished eating. I wondered if they only prayed aloud on Sundays. Another question I had but didn't have the opportunity to ask.

We cleaned up from breakfast while Caleb hitched up the buggy.

Mom gave Mary Esther a ride to church in her car. I decided to ride in the buggy with Beth, Joanna, Jonas, and Caleb. Rosie stayed home with the baby, and the rest of the girls walked to church.

Riding in the buggy was a terrifying but fun experience. Caleb made certain sounds, and the horse sped up with a jolt. Most of the ride to church was uphill, and I thought we were going to slide backward from the slush and ice, or get stuck. Those buggy wheels are so narrow...sometimes I was sure we were going to tip over. I held onto the seat with white knuckles, and Beth and Joanna playfully laughed with me at my nervousness.

When we arrived, Mom's bright red car stood out from the buggies like a ladybug among ants.

Most of the women wore light or dark blue dresses with buttons in the back. They wore white prayer *kapps* with black *kapps* over them. The black ones were designed to be worn outside. They also wore black sneakers or black boots.

(The finished church and school is pictured above.)

The church building looked like an unfinished house. The windows were not yet installed and were temporarily boarded up, but the wood stove kept the entire building relatively warm. There was a table where the women left their coats and bags.

Suddenly, several of the girls started chattering and pointing out the window. I looked out and saw a gray-haired woman trudging through waist-high snow toward the church, clearly on a mission, walking stick in hand. She finally came around the building and entered. Once she did, she came right up to me. I probably stood right out.

"You must be Ashley. Caleb told me about you. I'm his mother, Elizabeth. Welcome. It is so nice to meet you." She smiled at me, still catching her breath.

"It's nice to meet you. too. And now I have no excuse to ever miss church again after seeing you walking so far in such deep snow!"

The other women watched as Caleb's mother introduced herself to my mom. Then a line formed behind her. One by one each woman approached us to introduce themselves until we had met every female in the building. On Sundays the men and women sit separately and do not mingle, so we did not meet any of the men.

As I spoke to more and more people, I realized the Amish in Unity have an accent. Maybe it's more of a northern Maine accent—I'm not sure. They pronounce "really" like "reallay" and "family" like "familay" and they roll their L's a little. This became more apparent the more and more I spoke with the Amish.

We went downstairs for the church service. If I hadn't known from my research that men sit on the right side and women sit on the left, I might have accidentally sat with the men like my mom almost had. But I steered her to the women's side. I saw a hymnal with the last name of the family I was staying with written on it, and we sat there.

"The women sit in the back and the girls sit in the front usually, but you may sit wherever," said Caleb's mother. We stayed in that seat. As I waited, I looked around the room at the crowd of over seventy plainly dressed people.

Out of all of them, my mother and I were the only ones who owned cell phones. Isn't that something?

Service began, and we sang from the songbook. Most of the singing was in German. A man would call out a song number, and we would sing it—without instrumental accompaniment—while whoever chose the song led the singing. It was amazing how everyone kept time, stayed in tune, and sang perfectly together. They even harmonized. It sounded incredible in that small room. Out the window, the snow was piled high around pine trees. To me, it seemed too bad that we were so far out in the woods and no other people could hear the singing. It was one of the most beautiful sounds I have ever heard.

After we sang, everyone quickly stood and kneeled, facing their chair. I was expecting this, thanks to my research, and did the same as everyone else, but Mom remained seated, looking confused. No one seemed to notice or mind.

After prayer, Caleb gave the message. As you may have seen in Amish movies, usually Amish communities have a bishop. Because Unity is relatively new and small, the bishop travels between there and Smyrna, the Amish community in northern Maine.

He was not there that Sunday, and on the days he was not there they had one of the Amish men fill in as a speaker. That speaker was out of town, and I hadn't realized until then that Caleb would be filling in for that speaker.

Caleb led the service as the entire first chapter of Corinthians was read aloud by the men in the congregation. Each man took a turn reading.

The service was from 9:00 to 11:30 a.m. After, we ate a potluck lunch that all the women and girls set up. Caleb's family contributed the egg salad that I'd helped make. All the food was delicious. There were trays of sandwiches, meat pies, soups, casseroles, and plenty of baked goods.

After lunch, a young woman named Jolene talked to me for a while.

"So, what made you want to come here?" she asked.

"I want to write Amish novels and want to get to know the Amish so I can portray them accurately in my books. I want to see how you all live and experience it for myself. That way I can describe your lifestyle accurately in the books."

"That is great! I think not many writers do that. It's good that you are here to experience our lifestyle for yourself."

Again, relief and gratitude filled me.

"So what about you? Where do you live and what do you do?" I asked her, knowing she was clearly out of school.

"I live with Caleb's sister, Christina. I am the school teacher here," she told me.

I could tell she was not much older than me, and I was only twenty. "How old are you?"

She was twenty-two and had not gone to school beyond eighth grade, just like every other Amish student. My mother and I had the most education out of everyone in the community, and we had never even gone to college. We both had our cosmetology licenses, and I had a certificate in writing books, but no college degrees, and we still had the most education out of everyone there—even including the men.

After lunch, I met Caleb's sister, Christina, who invited me back to stay with her. I told her I would love to, and she gave me her phone number. She was lovely, and I hoped it would work out so I could come back to stay with her.

I talked to a woman about rumspringa, a time in a young Amish person's life when they are allowed to leave the community to try living outside the community.

"The Amish young adults in Unity do not do that because they all choose to remain Amish. It is a shock for them once they see the ways of the outside world. Sometimes they give in and become too involved with things like drugs and drinking. However, parents do not make their children remain Amish. It is up to the child. And most of them choose to stay. It is what they know," the woman told me. "Also, the Amish do not try to recruit people into joining. In fact, we discourage it. People who are not Amish—*Englishers*—may be able to live like us for a while, but then they give up because it is too hard. To be Amish, usually one has to be born Amish."

I, for one, could not live this way permanently. I would miss electricity, music, my laptop, my car and the fast-paced life I am used to. But the main character in my book *Amish Alias* does leave the modern lifestyle for an Amish lifestyle. I think some people could do it, but it is definitely not for me. Our conversation did give me some ideas for the book. My main character in the book is a talented piano player. Would she be willing to give up her beloved instrument in order to join the Amish who do not allow instruments?

The events of the day flooded my brain with thoughts and information. After saying goodbye to everyone, we had to go home because of the snow storm. We made it home safely before the snow came down hard.

I couldn't help but wonder when I could return to Unity again. The Amish had made a lasting impression on me. I envied their community and lifestyle.

Tuesday, October 18th, 2011

I called Christina, Caleb's sister, a few weeks ago and she just called me back today. They had gone to Tennessee for two weeks, and she had lost my number. She said she was hoping I would call and leave my number.

Good news—Christina is willing to host me. I will be returning to Unity on the 22nd, and I get to stay until the 28th. I am SO excited!

Saturday, October 22ⁿᵈ, 2011

Finally, my car was packed and I was ready to leave, excited to return to Unity for an entire week. When I left my house today, I shut my dress in the door on the way out. It made me laugh. I am not used to wearing clothes like this.

On the way to Unity, I realized I didn't know which house was Christina's. I had never learned that detail. I knew she lived behind Caleb, but there were three houses behind him. I would have called, but I figured Christina wouldn't get my phone message in time anyway, because they didn't have a phone in their house. They used the community's phone. Oh, well. I'm sure someone will help me once I get there.

Around 9:30 p.m., I drove down the lane past Caleb's house, hoping my headlights didn't wake anyone up. Getting there that late concerned me. Maybe no one would be around to help, after all.

One of the houses behind Caleb's was still lit. I assumed that was Christina's home and drove up the dirt driveway.

(Christina's house and barn are in the photo above from a distance. The photo below is of part of Christina's house.)

When Christina came out, holding her baby, Evangeline, and a battery-operated lantern, relief washed over me. It was her house after all.

"Hi," she said. "Did you find our house okay?"

"Yes. I didn't know which house was yours, but I guessed this one was it when I saw the light on. I'm so sorry I'm arriving so late at night. I wanted to come earlier, but I got out of work later than I thought I would. I hope I'm not keeping you up too late."

"It's okay. Don't worry about it. Come on inside."

I gathered up my bags, and we went inside. Christina's husband, Edward, and Damaris, their three-year-old daughter, waited for us in the living room. Christina gave me a quick tour of the house and told me to make myself at home.

It is very similar to Caleb's house in terms of style and décor. Their house is two stories, and Edward's parents live in the basement. This is very common among the Amish. They take care of their elderly parents instead of sending them to nursing homes.

When you first walk into the house, there is a room where everyone hangs up their jackets and takes off their shoes. Then beyond that room is the kitchen, complete with a wood stove. To the left is a sunroom with huge glass windows and a porch with solar panels. To the right is a hallway with the bathroom and the stairs. The guest bedrooms are upstairs.

(Above is Christina's kitchen. Again, sorry it is blurry. I probably also took it very quickly. Even though my friends didn't mind if I took pictures of their houses, I wanted to take the pictures as quickly as possible out of respect.)

Christina said breakfast was going to be at 7:00 a.m., then they all went to bed. I went upstairs and went to bed, too.

(Below is a photo of the room I stayed in with one of the battery-operated lanterns.)

Despite their gracious comments to the contrary, I felt bad for keeping them up late.

Sunday, October 23rd, 2011

That Sunday morning, we walked a mile or two uphill and through the woods to get to church. Again, just like I thought last time when I was here, I'll never have an excuse to skip church again. When we got there, some of the women recognized me, like Rosie, who shook my hand.

Unlike last time, the church building was now finished. The room where church was held was large and had wooden floors and walls, and several installed windows. Next to this room is the school room, which was closed off. Downstairs was where everyone ate after the service. Though it had not been cold during the church service last time, it was definitely warmer now. And now that I had already been to one of the church services here, I felt much more relaxed, knowing what to expect.

As I waited for the service to begin, I counted about seventy-five people in the church, made up of thirteen families. Half of the service was in German, but it had a lot of English words thrown in, so I could keep up pretty well. Christina helped translate, whispering the sentences in English as the speaker spoke in German.

We sang several songs, but I couldn't find where we were on the page until we sang the last song. They were all in German and were sung very, very slowly. They were the slowest songs I'd ever heard. Still, they sounded beautiful like last time.

In the back of the room, they had a small mattress where the parents let their kids sleep through the two-and-a-half-hour service. At one point there were six children on the mattress, all sound asleep facing different directions. They were all so well behaved.

I was happy when an elderly man, who I would later find out was Christina's father-in-law, started preaching in English. I could actually follow along, and his sermon was moving. It was actually quite similar to sermons I usually hear in church.

Church was from 9:00 to 11:30 a.m. When church was dismissed, more women came up to me and greeted me. A young woman named Lydia explained which children belonged to which families, and another girl named Ella Ruth invited me over to her house for the Singing that was later on. I accepted right away, since I missed out on the Singing last time because of the snow storm.

We went downstairs to eat lunch. The women set up lunch and made two large pots of coffee on a gas stove top. I talked with Regina and Cara, two girls I had stayed with in March, and then we ate lunch. The food was very similar to what we had last time.

I sat with Regina, Cara and some other girls. Most of the time they conversed in Pennsylvania Dutch, probably out of habit.

In the middle of the conversation, Regina said to the other girls in a hushed tone, "We should talk in English so Ashley understands."

"No, it's okay. I like to try to figure out what you're saying." Sometimes I could understand. I was recalling more and more German the more often I visited. The people here speak German half or most of the time, especially at home, but so many English words are thrown in that I can usually follow them. Damaris speaks German to me because she hasn't learned English yet, and now I can somewhat understand what she is saying. I know the words spiele (which means 'play' and is used frequently), *esse* (eat) and simple words like that which are said often. I wish I would have brought a German word book with me, but I am getting better. Maybe I learned German in school for a reason.

Despite my telling them it was okay to continue in German, to be polite, they continued in English. I'd have to practice more another time. But it was nice knowing exactly what was going on.

After everyone finished eating, the church sang the Lord's Prayer. All the girls then made an assembly line. By hand, we washed, dried, and put away the dishes of seventy-five or so people in about fifteen minutes.

I left with Ella Ruth to go get Caleb's daughters—who had already left—so we could go to the Singing. We walked back through the woods and talked about the dogs our families had.

We walked by a huge hole, and she told me it was an old manure pit they wanted to make into a pond for cutting ice to keep their food cold. That sounded really unsanitary to me, but I was too shy to say anything about it. They also plan to skate on it, and they go sledding down the huge hills in the winter.

We went to Caleb's, and I met a girl there named Sharon. She was very friendly and talkative. We were asked in advance to read a story or poem at the Singing, and I looked through my Bible for something. Regina, Sharon, Ella Ruth, and I took a pony wagon to Ella Ruth's house.

A pony wagon is like a buggy, except it is open, with no roof, pictured next.

Cars flew by and around us, and almost every driver waved politely. The girls talked with each other, and I leaned back on the pony wagon seat, thinking how content I was and hoping I could continue coming here after this week of research. I loved it here.

We arrived, and the horse walked right up to a post. One of the girls tied him to it, and then we went in the front room of the house. Everyone talked as Ella Ruth made popcorn in an old kettle on a gas stovetop.

When the popcorn was done, we sat around the large table in the kitchen. Ella Ruth put sour cream and onion flavored powder in the popcorn, and the popcorn was gone within minutes. I asked her if she had ever had popcorn with nutritional yeast in it. She said no, and some of the girls thought that was funny. It does sound weird, but it is actually really good.

Everyone got a song book that had mostly English songs, which I was happy about. First, we each went around the table and read a poem or story. When it was my turn, I explained that all I had with me was my

Bible and I read Psalm 96, and they liked that one. Ella Ruth read a funny story about a princess who couldn't cry then finally could when she smelled an onion. Many more poems were read around the table, and when everyone was done reading, we began singing.

Instead of going shopping, going to the movies, watching TV or playing video games, this is the type of things the Amish teens in Unity do for fun. One of us would choose a song and say the song number aloud. Everyone would find the page, and the girl who picked the song had to start singing it alone, to start it out so everyone could join in on the same key. This happened at the beginning of every verse, and that was how they all started and ended on the same key without instruments. When it was my turn, I lead all the other girls in singing "Take My Life and Let It Be." It was wonderful. They sang it beautifully.

After the Singing, Caleb's daughters brought me back to Christina's. Jolene's parents had arrived from Kentucky, along with her little brother, Anthony, and her sister, Sylvia. Jolene's parents had fourteen children. The family was very friendly and they engaged in many conversations with me.

Monday, October 24th, 2011

That morning, I wished I could take a picture of Damaris and Sylvia playing outside my window, because they were so adorable. I didn't because I would have felt bad about it, like I was invading their privacy.

Christina told me that all communities are different, but here they will not pose for pictures. A few times since I have been here I have wanted to take a picture of Amish people walking along the road, but I was afraid they would turn around and see me and not trust me anymore.

Christina said, "I don't mind if I'm driving down the road in my buggy and someone takes a picture of me, but I don't know how the others feel about it."

I decided to not take any photographs of them at all. However, they were fine with me taking pictures of objects like their houses, barns, and the scenery.

That morning, I went downstairs to help with breakfast. Jolene's mom introduced herself to me, saying she had never met an Ashley before. Ashley is such a common name, so that surprised me a little.

We had toast, eggs, cereal, and cookies I had brought. I'd never had cookies for breakfast in my life.

After we were done eating, Edward read from the book of Acts and we all kneeled at our chairs to pray.

I did the dishes with Jolene's mom, who was very amiable. We hit it off right away. "We will be traveling all the way back to Kentucky by bus. That's how we got here. I just hope we don't have a long layover in New York City. But everything happens for a reason," she said.

She told me a story about how they were once in a buggy and Sylvia wanted a drink, but the motion of the buggy kept sloshing the drink onto her, so they stopped while she drank. Then another buggy and a car passed each other on the road ahead at the same time. She said she was sure that if they wouldn't have stopped, there wouldn't have been enough room on the road for the two buggies and car. They would have all passed each other at once, and there probably would have been an accident.

At 9:00 a.m. we started to make lunch. Christina sang while she worked. It seemed as though everyone sang here all the time, and they all sang well. They sang while doing things around the house, while walking down the road, and just for fun.

They don't have radios or music on their phones, but music is still a huge part of their lives.

While lunch was cooking, I picked two big boxes of grapes off their stems, cleaned them, and put them into jars for canning. Christina would eventually use them for juice and jam. At one point, there was a hornet in the box, which I almost accidentally grabbed along with a handful of grapes. That doesn't happen when you shop in a store, but the food isn't as fresh then, either.

While we worked, Christina told me about how she met her husband, Edward. They grew up together and courted for a year or so until they were married when she was twenty-four. She had dated a few men and had received proposals, but she'd declined them. When Edward proposed, she knew he was the one for her. People often ask me if the Amish marry very young or have arranged marriages, and in Unity, that is not the case at all.

"What is the average age when people get married here?" I asked.

"Usually between twenty and twenty-five, or it could be older. Most people think the Amish marry very young, but the marrying age is generally the same age as non-Amish people. Dating in the Amish community is strictly hands-off—as in no physical contact of any kind until marriage, which even includes holding hands. Usually a courtship starts as 'dating,' where the couple may have a date once a month until they are engaged. When they are engaged, they can have a date once a week until they are married. Usually a couple does not date without serious intentions of marrying, and all Amish marriages last. There is no such thing as Amish divorce."

Jolene, the school teacher, was twenty-two and dating Christina's brother, Abner, who was twenty-five. Christina believed they would get married.

Another interesting fact is that when an Amish couple is married, they do not kiss at the altar because they believe it draws too much attention to them. After the ceremony, they have a big reception with lots of delicious Amish food. That part is similar to what I'm used to. However, our weddings are usually catered. The Amish do all the work themselves.

After a meal, all the men leave their dishes at the table exactly as they are, and they leave. They do not participate in meal preparation or clean up at all. Instead, while they are waiting, they read. The Amish read a lot, since they don't have TV. They read books just like us, as long as they are not immoral. However, I was flipping through a novel Christina recommended to me called *Tisha.* It was about a teacher in Alaska, and many of the words were crossed out. My guess was that they were profanity or words misusing God's name.

After we ate lunch, I washed the dishes while Christina pressure cooked and canned the grapes. I went to a deli down the road, bought two scoops of ice cream, plugged my phone into the wall, and waited there for an hour and a half while it charged. I found some nutritional yeast there and bought a container of it for Ella Ruth's popcorn so she could try it.

As I waited for my phone to charge, I wrote about my week. I hoped I could come back soon, and my mind began to wander. I decided to write my thoughts in my journal.

If Jolene marries Abner, I hope she invites me to the wedding. It is possible! I'd love to see an Amish wedding! When I get married, I want to invite them to my wedding, but I wonder if they would come because it would be so different from the weddings they are used to, and it would be such a long car trip to pay a driver for.

As for dancing, I always thought they were against all types of dancing, but Christina said mostly they are against couples dancing together, especially if they are unmarried. They don't mind children dancing at all or people dancing individually.

I really want to go teach the children at school some fun dancing that each person does individually, and Christina said she thought that would be fine.

As I wrote, I looked at my hands. I had grape debris stuck under all my nails. There certainly was no need to paint fingernails here. The Amish women were always getting their hands dirty, and they were not afraid of it. A manicure would have been pointless.

As I sat in the deli and watched people come and go, I realized I was so used to seeing long dresses, white bonnet-type head coverings, and men in suspenders that people in modern-looking clothes now seemed odd to me. When I was in Unity, I felt a little self-conscious for not wearing a head covering. But they did not expect me to act just like them. Now I felt self-conscious for not wearing my modern wardrobe. Strange how I immersed myself into the community in such a short time. I still wondered if the Amish were aware of their clothing when they went to town and if they cared. I'd have to remember to ask about that.

A few times so far, Christina had had to remind me no one expected me to dress and act just like them. She had even told me again when we were at church. I had hung up my white jacket among the dozens of black coats hung on the wall.

"I guess I brought the wrong color jacket." I just wanted to blend in as much as possible.

She said, "Don't worry. We do not expect you to do everything like us."

As I thought about my time in Unity and continued to write in my journal, I felt like we cooked and cleaned all day long. Every single meal was a big deal to the Amish. Each meal—with preparation, prayer and clean up—took us about two hours. Even breakfast was a big event. We made biscuits from scratch, cinnamon buns, pancakes...it was never boring.

I was so used to eating breakfasts that involve no cooking or cleaning. It saved so much time that way.

But the Amish believe mealtime should be bonding time. And maybe that is why they are so close. While I was there, I never saw any siblings argue. They all got along so well, like close friends. I never saw a child say or do anything disrespectful. It is not that they were all quiet and only spoke when they were spoken to. They were lively and happy, but they knew how important respect was.

But don't they get tired of all the work and wonder why they can't use modern conveniences to get it done quicker? Then they would have more time for worship, prayer, fun, and family time.

I had only been here a few days, and I felt like I spent most of my time cooking and doing dishes. At home, it took me only a few minutes to load up the dishwasher. Here, dishes took up a huge chunk of each day.

It all came back to the issue of contentment Christina told me about. They were content with what they had and the way things were.

I wondered how long I could happily live that way.

Tuesday, October 25th, 2011

This morning we had pancakes with sausage gravy, which I thought was really different. Who needs maple syrup when you have gravy?

After breakfast, I asked Jolene if I could teach art and dance at school. I explained to her that it was not partner dancing, and she was happy to have me do it. She told me to show up at 1:30 p.m. on Friday, then she left with her family for Acadia National Park, which is a 47,000-acre recreation area in Maine.

Esther, a woman who lived down the road in the house where the Singing had been held, invited me to her house. I got picked up at 8:30 a.m. that morning by her, her son Tim, and her four-year-old daughter Debra. They were on their way back from dropping some of their other children off at school. I brought along my art supplies and the nutritional yeast I bought for Ella Ruth. We drove to their house on a pony wagon with a cider press in the back. We had to walk at the end because it was too much for the pony to pull along with our weight up a small hill. Once we got off the wagon, the pony was able to pull it to their house.

At their house, I taught Debra and her two-year-old brother Seth how to paint. We colored paper over leaves with pastel watercolors. They loved it! I was a private art tutor for a few years, so I knew a few fun art projects I could teach them.

Ella Ruth, Maria, and Esther cooked and helped me make mozzarella cheese from scratch. They put some ingredients with milk in a big pot which I cut, stirred, and strained.

I gave Ella Ruth the yeast I had bought and she said she would make popcorn later so we could try it.

Ella Ruth asked me, "Do you have TV?"

"Yes, but I don't have time to watch it much. I'm so busy all the time." It was true. I hardly ever watched TV.

The other boys in the family came in, and we had rice with beef and vegetables, bread, a cantaloupe I had brought, watermelon, cake, and milk.

They almost always had dessert, which was always something homemade, with lunch and supper. I guess they needed the calories and burn it off with all the hard work they do.

They put their dessert—usually a baked good such as cake or pie— in a bowl and pour milk over it. I have never seen this before, and I thought it would taste weird at first, but it is actually really good.

These are Esther's twelve children in order of oldest to youngest:

Caroline

Joseph

James

Timothy

Ella Ruth

Maria

Lily

Laura

Rosanna

Naomi

Debra

Seth

Their house reminded me of the movie *Cheaper by the Dozen*, but not as chaotic. Because there was no electricity, the children entertained themselves. They were happy doing simple things. They worked a lot doing chores and went to school (except for the small children), but they also knew how to have fun playing board games, jumping rope, singing, or running around outside.

Afterward, the boys read books while we girls cleaned up.

Esther said, "There are so many dishes with such a large family, but that's what we are here for. Right, girls?"

I faked a smile, wondering what she meant by that. I didn't think girls were made to just do dishes and housework, but maybe I had misunderstood what she had said. Maybe she had meant it was only part of what they were made to do—I wasn't sure.

We washed all the dishes and then went back to painting and drawing. I drew a horse and they loved it. I taught them how to make origami paper frogs and how to cut a piece of paper a certain way that enables you to step through it.

They absolutely loved the paper frogs. We drew faces on them, and they enjoyed "feeding" each other's frogs by putting pieces of paper into the frogs' paper mouths.

The girls showed me the barn. It was huge! On the outside it looked like a huge greenhouse made of vinyl, and the roof was rounded instead of pointed.

They had cats, cows, horses, and enormous pigs. We went into a greenhouse where they stored peanuts and beans, and we shelled beans for a while and talked. I asked them questions, and they asked me questions, too.

Their peanuts in the greenhouse are pictured next.

"So what do you do for fun at home?" Maria asked me.

"My best friend and I get together a lot, and we like to go shopping or watch movies. We also dance together, so sometimes we choreograph new dance routines. I also write a lot, as you know, because that is my favorite thing to do. I also like to go out to eat with my friends and family."

"That sounds fun. Do you have a boyfriend?" Ella Ruth asked.

"No, not right now."

"What's your job like?" Maria asked. "Do you like it?"

"Well, I work at a busy salon. So I cut hair and color women's hair and do highlights. So I make their hair lighter or darker or put streaks in it. They call the salon and book appointments with me or sometimes I take people who walk in. But I also work at my mom's salon in her house. I like that a lot better because I make more money per service and I can work when I want to. One day I'm going to have my own salon in my house when I get married, I hope."

(Now I do have my own salon in my home since 2015.)

"Oh, wow! That would be so great to own your own business. Then you could be home with your children." Ella Ruth smiled.

"That's actually a big reason why I want to do it," I told her.

"Where did you go to high school? Did you go to college?" Ella Ruth asked.

"I was homeschooled until high school and then I went to a small Christian high school. I didn't go to college, only hair school for one year."

Afterward, I went with Maria to sweep their bike shop.

(Below is a photo of their sign.)

Then Lily, Rosanna, Naomi, and Laura came home from school. We played jump rope for about an hour, then we played limbo and the high jump. I tied the ends of the rope together to make one big circle, and we held on to it and ran around. Little Seth laughed so hard, which made all of us laugh.

We went inside, and I taught the rest of the kids painting as we ate popcorn with the yeast I had bought for Ella Ruth. It was great to see them all having so much fun and learning. They loved learning new games, so I taught them how to play the "clothespin game." It is a game where each person gets five clothespins, and someone picks a word you are not supposed to say. We chose the word "what." When someone says that word, the person who catches them takes one of their clothespins. Whoever has the most at the end wins. We laughed so much the entire time.

"Mom, what do you want me to put in the lunches?" Lily asked as she packed lunches. All at once several of the girls said, "You said it!" and tried to take one of her clothespins.

They started to use the German word for "what."

I said, "What is the word for it?" and one of the girls took one of my clothespins. We decided no one could say "what" in German either.

To trick the girls, I said, "Whoopie pie," and, "Walk," and "Won." Soon Esther started playing too. Sometimes the girls would say something quietly or mumble something to make another say, "What?" It was so hard to not say it! Even the older boys, who were usually very quiet and never spoke a word to me, laughed. Soon their father Irvin came home from work and asked what we were playing, smiling at our silliness.

Then we played a game called Evolution, which is much like Pictionary, except the pictures change from one thing to the next depending on your teammate guessing on what the picture is. I drew a moose that ended up being a chicken. The children laughed the entire time.

They showed me their rooms, and I told them about the books I've written. They were very interested in reading one of my other books, *Identity*, so maybe I'll send them a copy one day when it is published.

Wednesday, October 26th, 2011

The next morning, I awoke to a strange *tap tap tap* noise that ended with a *ding*.

That has to be a typewriter.

I woke up and looked around the guest room. It seems to me that almost every Amish home has at least one guest room. That interested me, given how large their families are. But I'm assuming it's because they are so hospitable and welcoming. And for that, I was grateful.

(Below is a picture of one of the bedrooms in Esther's house.)

The clacking and ringing continued, and I wandered downstairs to investigate. There sat Irvin at a desk, typing away.

"Good morning," he said.

"Good morning. What can I do to help?"

"You can mix this grape juice." Esther handed me a jar of purple liquid. "Mix it with a jar of water." Then she gave me a jar of Stevia, a non-sugar natural sweetener they love, and told me to put in one tablespoon. I mixed it for a few minutes as Debra climbed onto the counter and watched me. We poured it into cups as we waited for the biscuits to finish.

The younger children made even more paper frogs while waiting for breakfast. This time they taped strips of paper inside for tongues, which they found to be very silly. I had to agree.

Then we had morning devotions, which Irvin led. We read Matthew 6, which talks of how to pray and teaches the Lord's Prayer, and each person took turns reading a verse. Afterward, Irvin went around asking us what we thought of the passage.

My answer was, "Sometimes the good things you do in secret make more difference than the things done in the open."

He agreed, and the discussion continued. Then we went over the Lord's Prayer, and the oldest boy didn't know what "hallowed" meant.

"It means holy," I said quietly.

"What was that?" Irvin asked me.

"It means holy," I said, "Or separate, or sacred."

He looked slightly surprised that I knew this, but I didn't take offense. They didn't know everything about my culture just like I didn't know everything about theirs. Then Irvin asked the boy what the first part of the Lord's Prayer meant to him and what he thought, but the boy said he didn't know. To me, it means when we pray, we should acknowledge the holiness of God, just like in the first line of the Prayer. But I didn't say anything. Irvin talked with the boy about it for a moment, then we kneeled at our chairs to pray before we ate breakfast.

After breakfast, it was 7:45 a.m. and almost time to go. As the girls hitched up the pony, Esther asked me, "Is it very different here than what you expected?"

"The first time I came it was. When I first arrived in Unity, I had no idea what to expect. I didn't know you could have running water without electricity." I also thought they had outhouses, but I left that out. I chose only to mention a convenience or two, leaving out our feelings and beliefs. It still stuck with me that the girls thought they were born only for menial labor and nothing more, but I had no desire to get into a philosophical debate, particularly one that they might find offensive.

"Do you cut your hair?" She motioned to my long braid. "Or is it against your religion?"

"No, it's not against my religion to cut it. I just like long hair because I can do a lot of different hairstyles with it. I've had long hair most of my life, actually."

When it was time for the girls to leave for school and drop me off at Christina's, I thanked Esther, and she invited me back to do laundry with them tomorrow, which is a day-long event that I couldn't wait to experience. I climbed into the pony wagon with Rosanna, Laura, Naomi, and Lily—she drove the wagon and was twelve years old—and we took off with Maria on her bike beside us. Maria thought it was funny that I thought she was eighteen or nineteen when she was actually fourteen. They all just seem so much older and mature for their ages.

They taught me the spelling of their last name, which is very German sounding. It took me a few tries to say and spell it correctly. As we passed by on the wagon, people waved politely. Esther said they usually do. That simple gesture fascinated me. At home, people bustle about and barely acknowledge each other on the street. Of course, I don't know my whole community the way the Amish do, so that could have something to do with it. On the other hand, I have a feeling the Amish would be that friendly with strangers, too.

We went over all the siblings' ages and birthdays. Lily and Laura actually knew all the names and birthdays in their family, except for only a few birthdays. I told them I hardly know all of my siblings' ages and birthdays, and I have only five siblings.

"Do you want to see pictures of my family?"

"Yes," they all said.

"The pictures are on my phone. Is that okay?" I asked.

"Sure!" They all agreed. It surprised me that they are fine with looking at or using other people's phones, but they cannot own one of their own.

They loved the pictures of my twin sisters.

"Wow! They look so alike! And they look like you," Lily said.

I showed them pictures of my house, my whole family, and my friends. They liked to see what my home looked like. "Your house is so nice!"

By the time I had let them see all my pictures, we were at Edward and Christina's house.

"We're so glad you came over. We had a lot of fun!" Lily said.

"I'll try to come tomorrow to help you with laundry. I hope I can. Thanks so much for having me over."

"You're welcome. Bye," Maria waved and rode away on her bike.

"Bye," the other girls called.

I waved and went into Christina's house, and they drove their wagon down the lane.

Later that day, we drove to Christina's brother Andrew's house and stayed from 11:00 a.m. to 3:00 p.m., where a group gathered to make applesauce. Maria and Sharon were there, and I helped them pick apples to put in a huge container.

Andrew's family grew and picked the apples themselves. We washed them, cut them up, and boiled them. We didn't have to peel them, for which I was grateful. I helped Sharon put all the boiled apples into a device that was secured to a table. Hot juice splashed us occasionally as the juice dropped into a bucket while I guided it in with a spatula.

The apples were strained by the device and the peelings came out one side while the applesauce emptied into a bowl. While the liquid was still hot, they canned it. We made one hundred quarts of applesauce that afternoon for several families to share all year, which covered more than the entire kitchen table.

While we worked, the younger children busied themselves by looking at books and playing with homemade play dough. I read them a few stories. Again, even though several of them didn't know English yet, they seemed to understand. They nodded and giggled when I read the funny parts, and they pointed to the pictures. We read one of my favorites,

Frog and Toad, which is the first chapter book I ever read on my own when I was little.

I went back to helping with the apples. As Sharon and I strained the boiled fruit, she told me about her five brothers, including a little redheaded boy named Charles who entertained himself by pushing chairs around as we worked.

As the days pass, I am continually impressed by how well the children treat their siblings and parents and how well behaved they all are. I got the feeling I wouldn't witness any tantrums here.

As we continued to strain the apples, there was some commotion by the window near the porch. We gathered around the window to see what everyone was laughing at. Andrew's white turkeys jumped up on the porch and started pecking away at the buckets of apples. Sharon went out and scared them away, and we all giggled at her flapping her arms and yelling at them. The women cut off the bitten parts of the apples and used the rest for sauce.

Afterward, Christina, Damaris, Evangeline, and I drove to an old museum with Jolene, her brother Anthony, her sister Sylvia, and her parents. The yard was full of old stoves!

The front room of the museum did not look like a regular museum. When we first walked through the door, it looked like the inside of a house. There were newspaper articles on the walls about the museum and its owner, Joe.

(Below is the sign on the museum.)

We went into a large room with dozens of old stoves and a huge collection of goofy salt and pepper shakers.

Then we found a massive room with a high ceiling that was filled to the top with hundreds of toys. We noticed a switch on the wall that said "activate toys." When we flipped it, all the toys came to life. Music that sounded like a marching band blared as everything moved, twirled, or danced. There were dolls, puppets, trains, cars, and marionettes. Wooden planes with whirling propellers hung from the ceiling.

(Below is a photo of the room full of toys.)

We walked around the entire room, fascinated at the colorful and complex arrangements.

There was a bright red wooden train complete with a whistle. We laughed at the silly ostrich marionettes marching around in a circle—they were as tall as Damaris! We leaned over the side of a fenced-in area containing mini cars that zoomed around a racetrack, and I wondered who had made this amazing room.

Joe showed us all the old pianos, stoves—one was made sixteen years before Lincoln was president—cars, and other antique things.

There were rows and rows of player pianos. I sat down and began playing. (I took piano lessons for ten years.) We sang "God Bless America" and "Let It Snow," but Christina, Jolene, and her parents had never heard those songs before.

Joe said, "Sing with us anyway. Oh wait... Can you even read the lyrics?"

I looked at him, somewhat flabbergasted. Did he really think the Amish didn't know how to read?

My Amish friends remained unflustered. Christina simply said, "Yes, we read." I didn't understand how she wasn't offended. She just smiled at the man while I stared at him with wide eyes, shocked at both of them. Did non-Amish people often assume things like this about them, and the Amish were just used to it?

"Don't you only go to school a few years?" he asked.

I couldn't believe that a man who lived just down the road from several Amish families knew so little about them. Yes, maybe many people know the Amish only go to school until eighth grade. But eighth graders can read.

Amish people are not uneducated or illiterate. In fact, they speak, write, and read English more correctly than most people I know. Our society has grown so used to slang and incorrect English that we don't even realize we speak with incorrect grammar anymore. Sometimes, when someone does say something that is correct English, it sounds strange to us. For example, it should be "This is she" instead of "This is her," or "as I said" instead of "like I said."

"We go to school until eighth grade, but we all read and write well," Christina explained, voicing my thoughts.

"Oh, I'm sorry," Joe apologized. "I jumped to conclusions."

"It's okay. We don't expect people to know everything about the Amish way of life," Christina explained graciously.

We sang "The Old Rugged Cross" and my Amish friends knew that one.

Joe had a car used in the movie *Skylark,* the sequel to Sarah Plain *and Tall,* which is a movie I grew up watching. He assumed I was Amish, even after I told him I had seen the movie several times. He must not have realized that the Amish do not watch movies or TV.

He said, "Do you ladies have a ride home?"

"Yes," I said, "we have my car."

"You have a car?" His eyes widened and he chuckled.

I showed him my car keys. "Yes. I'm not Amish."

"You're not? But you are dressed like them."

"Well, I'm not wearing a head covering. I'm just visiting them."

Later, I helped Christina with dinner by slicing up some pears she had grown. Then she sent me downstairs in Edward's mother's part of the house to watch the milk on the stove and make sure it wouldn't boil. We were going to make hot chocolate. While the milk heated, I talked to Edward's mother about the museum and the things we saw there.

"The owner assumed that the Amish do not know how to read. Do people say things like that to you often?" I asked.

"Sometimes. *Englishers* sometimes assume things about us that are not true at all. But we are not bothered by it. Some people think we have arranged marriages, that we are a cult, or are not educated at all. I'm glad you are here putting in the effort to learn about our ways."

I smiled, amazed at her and Christina's attitude toward the situation.

The stove gave off a surprising amount of heat that filled the entire house. They didn't even need another source of heat.

The children knew to stay away from the stove, except Evangeline, who toddled a little too close to it sometimes. It sure was hot when I stood near it. It had been hot in the kitchen where we made applesauce yesterday, too, even though all the windows had been opened in the house.

I brought the milk up when it was ready, and we mixed in some store-bought hot chocolate mix. They do not make everything from scratch like many people think. They also buy products like cereal, toothpaste, crackers.

At dinner it was only me, Christina, Edward, Damaris, and Evangeline, so we had an unusually simple meal. We had the pears, the pineapple I had brought, and popcorn for supper. Edward left right after we ate because he had a phone appointment in the shanty to call his brother.

Christina asked me to play with the girls while she cleaned up. I taught Damaris how to paint while Evangeline sat in my lap. We painted a cat, a horse, and an overflowing bathtub. She was actually very good for her age. Again, all she said to me was *Ja*, but in Pennsylvania Dutch and German the J is pronounced like a Y.

Me: Do you want to paint?

Damaris: *Ja*.

Me: Do you want to paint a horse?

Damaris: *Ja*.

Me: What color?

Silence.

Me: How about blue?

Damaris: *Ja*.

All our conversations were like this—short and to the point, but we managed to communicate with each other pretty well without anyone translating for us.

Later on, Jolene and her family returned. They looked at my self-published book *Identity* that I had printed myself, and they thought it was great. Anthony was especially interested and asked if he could borrow it for the night, so I let him.

That night, as we all headed to our rooms for bed, I realized I had finally stopped habitually feeling around on the walls in the dark for light switches. I was getting used to having no electricity.

Thursday, October 27th, 2011

The next morning, Jolene's father, Mr. Baker, read the devotions. Anthony gave me back my book, saying he liked it. He had stayed up all night and read the whole thing.

However, he said the part about the time traveling was unrealistic. Of course time travel is unrealistic. That's the fun part about fiction. Sometimes it is very unrealistic. He also told me the way the main character thinks is a lot like how he thinks sometimes. Overall, he had obviously thought it was interesting enough to read in one night.

Jolene's mother, Mrs. Baker, did the dishes with me and told me how much she enjoyed getting to know me. She gave me their address so I can write to them. We got their luggage together and brought it out the door.

The Baker's driver arrived. The Amish commonly hire locals to drive them to where they need to go, like the bus station. A middle-aged woman in jeans came into the house and sat down at the table. I realized I was not the only non-Amish person who knew this family well as they started chatting. Edward's mother gave the driver a drink.

She introduced herself to me and then asked me all about who I was and why I was there. She told me she frequently drives the Amish who live around here. Later on, an Amish family told me she does it in exchange only for some home-cooked Amish food instead of money. That's how good their food is.

The Bakers said goodbye to me, and Mrs. Baker gave me a big hug. "It makes me sad when I get to know someone and then realize I will probably never see them again. May God guide us both, for eternity is so long."

I wiped away a tear as they walked out the door. I was moved by her words and hated to see her leave.

We loaded up the driver's truck, and the Bakers set off on their two- or three-day journey back to Kentucky.

Afterward, Christina took me outside to see the ice house.

It is located on the side of the house behind a removable door. It is probably the size of my kitchen or larger, is made out of cement, and has a high ceiling.

"In the summer it has more ice in it, but this is what we have for now," she told me. The floor was almost covered in large blocks of ice that were about one or two feet long and one or two feet high.

This is where they store their perishable food.

We went back inside and I played with Damaris and Evangeline while Christina cleaned. As I played with the children, I talked to Edward's mom about my book *Identity*. She said she had read some of it. She also liked the *Chronicles of Narnia,* Tolstoy, *Lord of the Rings,* and the book Christina's father Elmo had written called *Give Me This Mountain.*

She told of a story in the book about a boy who received a nice new buggy that he loved, but then he purposely damages it. Halfway through, when the boy smashed the buggy's lights and slashed the seats, the author said that is how youths treat their bodies by drinking, doing drugs, and not practicing abstinence. It was a fascinating premise.

I told her about the Amish books that got me interested in learning about the Amish and coming to Unity. I then asked about bikes, because one book described the bishop banning bikes in an Amish community, but in Unity it was allowed.

"See?" she said. "Not all Amish are the same."

I told her in movies the head coverings are different looking. I saw a movie called *The Shunning,* set in Lancaster County. She showed me a book called *Just Like Mama*, also set in Lancaster. Edward's mother liked the pictures because they are accurate. She told me the head coverings in Lancaster are more heart-shaped, the women twist their hair on the sides, and they wear pink dresses.

The head coverings here are simpler. The backs have a round shape and there are eight pleats on each side. It is so interesting to me how each community is different in their styles of clothing, the way they speak, and their rules.

One of their prayer *kapps* is pictured above.

I read Damaris and Evangeline a few books until we sat down to eat. Christina made a casserole—they make a lot of those, and they are all so good—layered with moose meat and pork on the bottom, salsa, sour cream, cheese, and then a biscuit layer on the top. It was one of my favorite things I had there. And there was applesauce—but not the applesauce I had helped make—and cinnamon buns.

After we finished, I left to go to the store to get more dish soap and some fruit for Christina. She wanted to make a fruit pizza.

Then I drove to Ella Ruth's house, but I could see right away from all the clothes on the clothesline that they had finished with the laundry already. I went in anyway and sat on the couch with Esther, Seth, and Debra as Esther looked at a magazine with them and talked in German about the pictures. I learned new words by seeing her point to the pictures and say what was in them. Between what people have taught me and by listening, I can somewhat converse and say simple phrases, especially with the children who only speak German/Pennsylvania Dutch. I can tell the kids to come eat or ask them what something is.

As we looked at the magazine, I helped Debra string Cheerios for Seth to eat. Esther said all her kids liked to do that at one point. I've never heard of it, but it was fun. It reminded me of stringing popcorn for Christmas trees.

I went outside with Maria, Laura and Debra to the greenhouse. We picked peanuts off plants for an hour or two and played the clothespin game. We chose the words "that" and "the." That was hard. We said those words all the time and didn't even realize it.

I took pictures of the peanuts they grew and picked themselves. There were four big shelves full of them. We had two buckets full of peanuts at the end. To me, that did not seem like much from all those plants, but they told me that it was a good amount.

After, I helped in the kitchen by making apple dumplings. The girls peeled apples and ate some of the peelings.

I said, "If you like the peelings, then why do you peel the apples?"

"They taste so much better in the dumplings when the apples are peeled," Laura said.

After I took a bite of the apple dumplings I said, "You're right! It would not be as good with the peelings on."

This is a similar recipe to what we used. Of course, we had to double it to feed the large family.

Ingredients:

2 cups of flour

A teaspoon of cinnamon

A half cup of apple juice

One cup of diced apples

One tablespoon of cornstarch

Two 46 ounce cans of apple juice

Directions:

In a medium bowl, mix the flour, cinnamon, and one-half cup of apple juice. Stir until smooth. Mix in apples. Pour all apple juice into a pot with a tight lid and bring to a boil over medium heat. Mix in diced apples, cover pot and let it boil for twenty minutes. It is important to not remove the lid during this time. After the twenty minutes are up, remove the dumplings from the pan and set aside. Stir cornstarch into remaining apple juice in the pot and cook until it is thick. Serve over dumplings.

Makes 8 servings. May serve immediately (plain, with milk, or with ice cream) or allow to cool.

(We ate ours with milk on it, of course.)

As I swept the remaining apple peelings off the floor and washed dishes, Esther asked me if I had a dishwasher.

I said, "Yes, but sometimes it doesn't work well. I'm used to doing dishes by hand."

She said it was refreshing to see a young person who is not Amish willing to work. I just liked to help.

"I get the impression from what people say that young adult *Englishers* can sometimes be disrespectful or lazy. Do you think that is true?" she asked.

"Well, all the teens I know are very respectful and are good workers. But I bet there are many teens who are not like that."

"Well, I do not know many teens who are not Amish, so I wouldn't know."

I knew she wasn't trying to insult our culture. I just hoped I was setting a good example.

As we washed dishes from baking, I ended up accidentally spraying myself with the sink hose. Rosanna giggled with me at my clumsiness.

For dinner, we had a really good stew Ella Ruth made with chicken, vegetables, gravy, and stuffing. There was also white cabbage coleslaw that looked like grated cheese. Then we had the apple dumplings, and they were delicious.

As we cleaned up the dishes from dinner, a rubber band fight started. They ducked and ran and fired bands at each other, running around the house, laughing hysterically the whole time. This was the first time I had seen the children make a lot of noise.

Lily asked me above the chaos, "Does it get this crazy at your house?"

"Sometimes. But we don't have quite as many people at my house. Sometimes when we have friends over it gets this loud."

She said with a laugh, "We have so many people here, we don't need to have friends over to have fun!"

Once the "fight" died down, we drew pictures and painted at the table. I drew the profiles of Lily, Ella Ruth, Maria, Rosanna, and Naomi.

The children were amazed at how some of the pictures closely resembled them.

Friday, October 28th, 2011

This morning we ate breakfast and I did the dishes again. Christina told me she was going to do laundry, and I was so excited to help her because I had missed out on helping the family of twelve the day before.

Washing clothes took a long time. They used an old-fashioned Maytag washer run by gas that swished the clothes back and forth, and then they put it through a wringer that squeezed most of the water out. We rinsed it in a bucket and sent it through the wringer again, then hung out on the clothesline. I was afraid my fingers would get caught in the wringer, which could have happened if I was not careful.

(Below is a photo of the washer we used.)

After my stay with the Amish, a few people told me stories of people they knew that got their arms caught in it. There is a button to push that opens the contraption if that does happen, but I didn't want to find out what that would be like.

After the laundry was done and hung on the clothesline, I packed up everything to bring out to my car so I would be ready to go. As I walked out the door to bring my duffle bag to the car, Damaris saw me with my bags and she started to cry.

"I'm not leaving yet," I told her. "I'll be right back."

Christina held her and comforted her. She looked at me with a smile and said, "She'll be okay in a minute. She's grown attached to you."

I had really bonded with the little girl over the week, even though she was rather shy and we speak different languages. I had read to her whenever she brought a book to me, and I had played with her and Evangeline while Christina was busy. Now I felt sad to get to know her so well only to leave her, but I knew I would come back here soon.

I went back to the museum and took dozens of pictures of all the stoves and the room full of toys, and I found Joe puttering around in his wheelchair. I asked him if he would take a picture with me and he asked one of his workers to take it, telling me he was somewhat camera shy.

After we took the picture, he told me he was going to Florida for the winter, but the museum would stay open all year long. He said he hoped to see me there again someday, and I told him that was very possible.

Next, I drove to Lydia's house for lunch. She and her big dog came out to greet me. Her sister Tabitha and her mother Katie were inside. They own a bakery where they bake from 5:00 a.m. to noon every Thursday and Friday to sell their goods at a market on Saturday.

(Below is their house.)

Their bakery is open all week though, I think. It is located in a building right next to their house. They make whole wheat breads, pies, rolls, turnovers, and the like. They have an oven with multiple doors and compartments where they bake several things at once.

When I got there, I helped them make blueberry turnovers. It was a time-consuming process. There were lots of dirty dishes to wash.

Lydia's father and brother came in. We sat down and had the silent prayer. He asked me about myself, and somehow the dinner conversation turned to Noah's Ark. I told them about a church sign I saw once that said, "Where did Noah put the woodpeckers?" They thought that was pretty funny, as I had when I had first seen it.

For lunch we had noodles they had made from scratch along with salad and bread that had also been made from scratch. I would have enjoyed helping make the noodles and bread, but I hadn't been there to assist them.

After lunch, I had to leave right away to make it to the schoolhouse in time, but not before I bought three turnovers and four pecan rolls to bring home to my family. I arrived at the school at 1:20 p.m., just in time to teach at 1:30 p.m.

When I walked through the doorway of the classroom, all the children looked at me but didn't make a peep. Jolene had me sit on the side of the room while they did spelling.

The school room looked like any other classroom, except for the clothing the students wore, of course. The walls were decorated with colorful art work, and there were posters and a big chalkboard. Jolene had her own desk, and each student had a desk like the ones in modern public schools. There were about twenty-three children in the class.

They do not take time off for holidays, but they do for an occasional wedding. Their summer break starts in April and ends in September. Without holidays, they get things done faster, and they are all extremely well behaved in class, so maybe at eighth grade they are very much ahead of their eighth grade public school counterparts.

The Amish only go to school until eighth grade because they believe further education is prideful. The children are also needed at home to work, because chores take longer with many kids and animals and no electricity. People might say the lack of electricity robs the children of a proper education, but all the Amish families I have met own successful businesses and are content with their level of schooling. Quite frankly, they are content with everything.

Irvin owns a windmill company and his boys have a bike shop where they sell bikes and do repairs. Lydia's dad makes furniture, and her family owns a bakery. Caleb has a store, and he and Edward sell their produce.

For them, high school is unnecessary. They don't need to make a lot of money and the women seem happy to stay home and work and take care of the children.

It's like what Christina was saying about contentment. They are content with simple lives and they seem as happy, or even happier than any other people I know. Their families are close and they stay together. They respect each other and all get along.

For them life is about faith, family, food, work, and fun.

I saw first-hand their love of family, so I had no doubts about that. But I wondered about their faith. Did some of them just follow the customs because that's all they knew? Or because they were expected to. Or for fear of being shunned? Or did they really believe the tenets of their faith? Did they just hope they'll go to heaven, or did they fervently believe their lifestyle would get them there? I wondered if they suffered crises of faith like people of other religions sometimes do.

Their faith certainly did seem genuine—each and every one of them. I supposed it had to be to live in such a way.

One of the things that interested me the most about their faith was that they didn't evangelize. But I remember the Amish woman from church telling me that most Amish are born into it. Very few outsiders join the Amish and fewer end up staying.

Perhaps that's why they didn't evangelize. No point in trying to get someone to join your faith if you don't expect them to be able to last in it. I don't, however, think they are completely against evangelism, because Christina asked me if I evangelized at work. I hoped I showed them not all non-Amish were the same. I hoped I was a good example of non-Amish Christians.

Jolene finished up spelling with the class and then introduced me to them. Next was recess. I told them whoever wanted to could come with me and I would teach them exercises and stretching outside.

Most of the girls joined me while the boys were a little more hesitant. We did some simple stretching and jumping. The girls stood in front of me while the boys watched sheepishly off to the side. I told them to start off by doing jumping jacks, but not one of them knew how to do it. I couldn't believe it.

While we jumped, they laughed the whole time, saying it was silly and funny, probably feeling self-conscious. I even had them hop around in a circle on one foot, and they laughed even harder. Then they surprised me by asking me to teach them a dance. So, I taught them parts of the hip hop and jazz dances I was learning that year. They did quite well learning them, and they laughed at the dancing, too.

After we went inside, I taught all the children how to make paper frogs. Many of the children asked me to draw faces on them. After all the frogs were done and everyone was dismissed, I asked Jolene how she kept the class so quiet.

"They just know they are not supposed to talk until they are called on," she said simply, like it was obvious.

"Well, what if they do?"

"I suppose they would get in trouble, but it never happens. They are taught at home to not talk in class until they are called on."

"I wish I could get my dance students to be that quiet in my class," I told her, laughing.

On my way out, a few of the children asked me to go to their houses, but I told them I had to go home, but I would come back in the winter or spring. They thanked me for teaching them, and I got in my car.

Back at Christina's house, she asked me how teaching went and I told her how they laughed at the ballet dancing, and she asked me to show it to her. She thought it was quite interesting. She had probably never seen anything like that before.

I wrote down my address for them and hugged Christina and Evangeline goodbye. I knew I would miss them. I thanked Christina over and over for having me, and she told me I was welcome back.

Before I left, Christina gave me a copy of a book that her father Elmo wrote before he died—*Give Me This Mountain: A Selection of Views and Values*. It is a collection of short stories. He had written stories and articles for a magazine and collected them all to compile into a book. His book was written on a typewriter, and his mother said he typed out several versions of it before it was published. They probably have a limited number of copies, so the book was a precious gift. What she wrote in it was even more precious:

To my friend Ashley,

I've enjoyed spending time with you this week. I pray God will supply your every need and bless you!

Love, Christina and family.

During my visit to Unity I realized how much I respect the Amish.

People think they are quaint, but they know so much about the world, and living their lives is hard work. It takes so long just for them to go somewhere nearby.

I love the freedom of owning a car. I was happy to drive around after not driving for a few days. However, my week there had been so fun. I had the best time with them, and I felt so blessed to have experienced something so incredible.

I think I could live like them for a few weeks or even a few months, and then I would miss my phone, car, and laptop. I wouldn't like to do my writing with a typewriter like Elmo did. I would really miss my laptop. Even if it is a hunk of junk.

However, I barely noticed not having electric lights after a few days, and since the house is heated by the wood stove, the only electronic household appliances I think I'd really miss would be a microwave, a fridge, and outlets to charge things with.

I am really becoming more thankful for the life I have. There is so much work the Amish have to do. I think—and I could be wrong—that they don't really see chores as just doing chores. I think they view chores as another way of serving God by feeding, clothing, and caring for others.

To me, I have much more time to serve God living the way I do without having to spend extra hours doing chores the long way, and I am content with the life I have. However, living with the Amish has made me want to become closer to God, and I am planning on doing just that. It is something that does not happen overnight—it takes work, prayer, and studying the Bible. The Amish certainly know a lot about that.

I went to Unity to do research and learn about the Amish, but really I have learned a lot about myself, and I have made good friends there. I know the Amish of Unity see me as a friend, because they have told me I am welcome to come back any time.

I decided to leave the copy of *Identity* behind so my friends in Unity could read it and pass it on. I wrote an inscription in it before I left.

To my friends in Unity:

Thank you for a fun learning experience. I learned more than I thought I would… Not just about facts, but about your kindness and love and friendship, and about God and myself. I will always remember this week and be grateful for it.

Love,

Ashley.

Letters to and from the Amish

(Some are abridged to leave out personal information.)

10.7.11

Dear Christina and Edward and family,

Thank you so much for letting me stay with you. It was one of the best weeks of my life, and I did not want to go back home! That transition back into my fast-paced life was a little strange at first, and I miss the quietness and peace of Unity. Everyone here was eager to hear about and learn about my stay with the Amish. They were fascinated, and some even said they would like to go for a week. They were impressed that I went a whole week without power. When I got home, there was a snowstorm, and many people lost electricity and were very disconcerted. Some people went a few days without power, and when I said I just went a week without it, they couldn't believe it! It's hard to go a few days without it for some people when they have lived their whole lives using it every day, I guess.

In my week in Unity, I realized life is so much more than electricity and clothes and money. These are just things we don't need. I learned that life is about worshipping God through loving people, working hard, and having fun. I wish life was that simple here where I live. Sometimes I think I can see a glimpse of it when people help each other or sing in church.

Anyway, I plan to come back between February and April of next year! I wish you all a safe winter. It is still very warm here, and sometimes it feels like spring even though we had a snowstorm recently. I hope it will be a mild winter for everyone.

I am looking forward to my next visit with you very much. I have been reading the book your father wrote, Christina, Give Me This Mountain. My mom is reading it, too, and we enjoy it very much.

I will bring/mail you a copy of the book I am writing about my week with you. It is almost finished!

Again, thank you so much for the memorable week and your friendship.

-Ashley

P.S. What process would one go through to join your Amish community? I was just wondering. Thanks!

October 16th, 2011

Dear Baker family,

I very much enjoyed getting to know your family during my stay with Christina and Edward. How was your trip back to Kentucky? I prayed for a safe journey for you. How long did it take to get there by bus? Did you have any layovers?

I appreciate Anthony taking the time to read my book, Identity. *I left it behind for whoever else wants to read it.*

Going to the museum with you was very fun! I also enjoyed getting to know Jolene. She let me go to school that Friday and teach the children art and outdoor activities at recess. They are very good learners! Jolene really does a good job at keeping the class in order. It is the most well behaved class I have ever seen. She is a very good teacher.

Thank you for a fun week. It was fun learning from each other. And thank you for your friendship!

-Ashley

October 7th, 2011

Dear Esther and Irvin and family,

I had so much fun with all of you! My mom was so impressed that I made cheese! I had so much fun playing with all you girls and teaching you art at your house. It was also very fun to go to your school. You are all very good learners.

I miss Unity very much. Sometimes when I drive around Biddeford and Kennebunk, I see fields with barns and pretend I am in Unity for a minute.

Thank you so much for inviting me into your home. I had so much fun, and I laughed more than I have in a long time! Whenever I see a clothespin, I will think of you girls.

I left a copy of Identity *with Christina for anyone who wants to read it. I will also mail/bring you a copy of my book I wrote about my week in Unity. It is almost done.*

Again, thanks so much for an unforgettable week. I hope to see you all again soon!

-Ashley

(On the back of this letter I drew a cat that looked like the cat we drew when we played Evolution. I also drew some of the paper frogs we made.)

November 2011

Dear Friend Ashley,

Greetings in love of Jesus' name. How are you and your family? Thank you for your letter. Yes, we had a safe journey home, much to be thankful for.

We didn't see snow in Maine, but I had wished to see some on the evergreens there. I love evergreens. But when we got to Boston, it started snowing and then in Pennsylvania it turned out we got 7 or 8 inches. So that was different for October, not even Halloween.

We are building a new house. The blocks are being laid, but now it is rainy today, and it's supposed to rain tomorrow—so it's on hold.

Our son, Raymond, shot a big buck, a 10-pointer. It is 220 pounds. So we had bologna made and it is good.

Yes, we want to appreciate our schools a lot, for it is so worthwhile. Our son, Lincoln, is not in a plain church, but his girlfriend Tanya is an art teacher and she cannot make her pupils do a thing. She may not even lay her hands on them to restrain them from hurting the others. She is teaching at a different school this year, as she has gotten convictions to wear a head covering and this school is so much better. But she still longs over the poor little children that she used to teach—those who are being drawn into evil through their parents.

Tomorrow we plan to shop at a place called "Habitat for Humanity." It's a thrift shop for builders. When one builds a house, there are so many small and large things to buy. It is interesting. We have built two houses before—one in Pennsylvania and one in Montana.

So have you found anything edifying in your visit in Unity? Would you consider living that lifestyle? It really isn't so hard. We have it pretty good compared with poor folks in many other countries. We likely don't do enough to help them. But we will sometimes do some volunteer work for CAM if there are disasters close by like tornados, floods, etc.

Our sons enjoy helping.

Well, I will close. I wanted you to know that I will remember you and I care about you—it was interesting to meet you.

May God guide us both, for eternity is so long...
Love, Mrs. Baker

December 2011

Dear Mrs. Baker,

It has been very busy around here! I am getting my wisdom teeth extracted on February 6. Do the Amish also have surgeries like that and/or go to the doctor for check-ups?

I am so glad to hear you got home safely. What a warm winter we have had here so far until very recently! In fact, sometimes I check the weather in California and it has been ten degrees warmer here in December.

Congratulations to your son Raymond on his buck! I don't know much about deer, but his deer sounds impressive to me. My dad also got a deer. He saw it early one morning in the back yard while he was drinking his coffee. He ran outside in his pajamas with his gun and shot it from our porch! It is a funny story we love to tell. He didn't even have to go in the woods. My mom made a very good stew out of it.

I have heard of "Habitat for Humanity" but I never really knew what it was. How amazing that you built 2 houses before and God supplied all the material. How is the building coming along?

I really loved going to Unity and I will hopefully return in February or March. I really do miss it there, and I actually did consider what it would be like to join the Amish church. I think I could do it, but I don't think it is meant for me. I heard many Amish people say you usually have to be born Amish to be Amish. I don't mind all the work (it's not much different than at home except for the laundry part) and I love the church and prayers and community. I believe mostly the same things the Amish believe. Everyone is very friendly and the families are close.

They all get along so well. That is a precious thing. I miss the peacefulness there. Life is so fast-paced here, sometimes I wish it would all slow down. Time seemed to stand still in Unity.

I love God with my whole heart, but I believe I am called to serve where I live. Lately I have been working in the church nursery and teaching Sunday School for the children. I also lead in the young adult ministry, which I love.

You are very right when you say you have it better than many people. There certainly was no shortage of food as far as I could tell! And it was all so delicious. I sponsor and send money to a girl in Uganda named Emily. She bought one fourth of an acre of a banana plantation with the $75 I sent her!

If I lived an Amish life, I know I would definitely miss my family. I would miss my car, a microwave, and my cellular phone. Also, writing books would be so much more difficult for me to do without my computer, and I have always known I am meant to write books.

I found it all so interesting in Unity, and so have so many people back here at home. Dozens of people have bought my book so far. They all are amazed with the story of my stay in Unity and all the things that happened. I sold almost all the copies I had, but I will order some more and send one to you and your family!

Thank you so much for your letter. You are the first and the only one to respond so far. (I sent out one to Christina and Edward and one to Esther and Irvin.)

It was so wonderful to get to know you and everyone in Unity. May God keep you all safe this winter!

Love, Ashley

December 31, 2011

Dear friend Ashley,

It's so hard to believe this is the last day of the year. It's thirty degrees and raining so there's some ice, but hopefully it will keep warming up so road conditions won't get too bad. It's a perfect day to just stay home by the woodstove and listen to the sound of the rain pattering on the roof. I'm so glad for the cheery sunroom with lots of windows on a day like this. The sky is gray with a mist hanging low over the soggy landscape.

I'm hoping and praying for safe traveling for the vanload heading to Ontario today. Caleb, Cara, Beth, Joanna, Jonas, my mother, and Simon (my cousin) are the ones who went. They plan to be gone for almost a week.

Thank you for the nice letter we received a while back. I apologize for not responding sooner. December was so busy, sometimes it seemed hard to keep up. I had very little spare time for letter writing. We also enjoyed your visit here, and I thank you again for being so cheery and helpful with the food you brought. I'm glad you found your time here worthwhile.

I guess you're probably also enjoying the mild weather this winter where you live. We have had some snow and a few storms, but overall it hasn't seemed like much of a real winter yet. But there is still time for that before spring comes. I'm glad to have winter shortened a little.

Damaris and Evangeline both have colds, which I'm really hoping they'll get over soon. It's hard to keep a child's nose clean when it is so runny. Besides, a cold can make one feel downright miserable, especially a stuffy head cold where one's sinuses make you feel like you're suffocating.

I'm becoming quite interested in growing herbs to make my own home remedies for my family. I wish I had more for this winter's colds and flus, but I have been giving the girls some grape juice with Echinacea mixed in and some elderberry and honey syrup that I think helped relieve their colds somewhat.

Two weeks ago we traveled to Smyrna for a four-day visit to help a family with a butchering project. Edward and his brother and some others killed, gutted, scalded, and scraped 12 hogs and 1 cow for about a half dozen households. Then we cut up some of those to make sausage, hams, bacon, and steaks, and the fat was rendered for lard. The bones were cooked in a big kettle, then scrapple was made with the broth, meat scraps, organ meat, corn meal, flour, and seasonings. I wonder if you know what scrapple is. I wasn't used to eating it before I got married, but I've learned to like it quite well. We eat it for breakfast with eggs, maple syrup, or apple butter.

I hardly know where to begin to answer your question about the process required to join an Amish community. In one way it is just as simple as going to a community and saying, "Here I am. I want to be a part of your community. I am here to learn and help." But on the other hand, if I would try to define all the adjustments a person goes through in the process of "pulling out of society" and blending into a plain community, it could sound pretty complicated. Of course, the biggest requirement in actually becoming part of a group is sharing the same faith and values. Faith in God and Jesus and a dedication to taking the Bible very seriously and being willing to let it order your life is a must.

I'm really looking forward to reading your latest book. I'm curious whether you took your visit here as the basis then wrote a novel with fictitious characters or if you did it like a diary or what approach you took to your "Amish Story."

You probably remember that Caleb's wife Rosie and Irvin's wife Esther are sisters. A few weeks ago they received the unexpected news that their father, who lived in Indiana, passed away. So Irvin's family and Caleb's family and other relatives from here and in Smyrna were gone for several days over the time of his funeral. I took Regina's place as the teacher at the school for two days while she was absent. I enjoyed the chance to teach again, but two days was long enough. I was glad to get back to being a stay-at-home wife and mother. Edward's mom and my mom helped Edward with caring for the girls so they didn't really mind my being gone much, but I still wouldn't want to do it often. I can't imagine having to leave them at a daycare center like a lot of mothers do in society.

Well, I'll close with wishing you a healthy, happy winter.

Love,

Christina, Edward, Damaris, and Evangeline

January 30th, 2012

Dear Christina, Edward, Damaris, and Evangeline,

This winter has been surprisingly warm! We have had a few storms, but it is not nearly as bad as some of the winters we have had before.

I hope you are all in good health. The flu and colds have been circulating through my home and at work, but thankfully I have not gotten sick yet.

I think the butchering project you mentioned in your letter was very interesting! That is a lot of meat! We get a side of beef from the farmer down the road who hays our fields. We also get raw milk from him. We still have moose meat from my dad's moose, and with that we make moose burgers and moose chili.

About the book... Tonight or tomorrow I will order some more copies. They have sold so quickly! I will bring them to you when I visit again in spring 2012.

I did not realize Rosie and Esther are sisters. I am so sorry to hear about their father. It is always so hard to lose a family member. But it is good to take comfort in knowing they are in the Lord's hands.

Were you a teacher before you were married? I didn't know that! When was that and for how long did you teach? How wonderful that you got to do it again. What an excellent group of scholars those children are!

Well, I close, praying for your health for the rest of the winter. Mrs. Baker and I have exchanged letters, and I sent one to Esther and Irvin's family. Tell them I said hi if you see them. I miss you all, and I will see you again soon!

God bless!

-Ashley

P.S. I have never heard of scrapple!

(On the back of the letter I drew a squirrel who eats near my house.)

****

(Below is a photo of some quilts for sale in a shop in Lancaster, Pennsylvania. They sell for about $1,000. Aren't they amazing!?)

(One of the stoves from a museum near the Amish community.)

Part 2

Attending an Amish Wedding

June 2012

About two months ago, I was surprised to receive a phone call.

"Ashley? This is Christina," my Amish friend said when I answered the phone.

"Hi! How are you? I'm so glad to hear from you." Knowing they don't have phones in their house, I asked, "Are you calling from the phone shanty? Or maybe from the store?"

"Yes, I'm calling from the shanty. I'm doing well, thanks, and so are the kids. You should be getting something in the mail soon. It's a wedding invitation to Jolene and Abner's wedding."

"Wow! That's wonderful. I'm invited?"

"Of course. We'd all love to see you there."

"I can't wait to see you all again."

I was so honored to be invited. I'd only known them for a short while, but I felt like I'd known them my entire life. Amish weddings are very different from ours, and I couldn't wait to experience it.

At that time, I worked at a local hair salon, and I got the time off work. My mom was supposed to go to Unity with me, but on the day before I was supposed to leave, she realized she couldn't come. I could have gone alone, but I wanted to share this unique opportunity with someone. So, I started my one-day search. I made a post on Facebook and went through my cell phone contacts, texting everyone I knew and their children who might be interested in going. Finally, after several people said "no" because it was so last minute, I got a "yes" from Hailey, who was twelve at the time.

Hailey was one of the dancers I taught that year at the dance studio where I worked. In fact, I taught her and her sister a private lyrical duet class. Her mother agreed to let her go with me. We made the plans, and I picked her up at 11:30 the next morning.

On the way to Unity, I explained everything I could possibly think of that she would need to know about the Amish during our stay. "They mostly speak German in the home and the children do not learn English until they go to school. At church, they greet each other with a holy kiss at church because the Bible says to, so don't be too surprised when you see it. The men kiss other men on the lips and the women kiss other women on the lips."

"That's so weird!" she said, laughing.

"It's how they do things. Also, sometimes they pray silently at meals, and sometimes they pray out loud." I told her everything that had surprised my mother when she had gone with me before my week-long stay. "We even brought our own toilet paper because we weren't sure if they'd use it, but they have indoor toilets and showers."

Hailey asked, "Do they have electricity, or TV, or Internet?"

"Nope."

"Then what will I do for two whole days?" she asked, holding her portable music player.

"Don't worry. We will be so busy you won't even think about it."

This twelve-year-old was sure in for a culture shock. What would she think of the Amish way of life? Hopefully she'd take it all in and learn something along the way.

As we approached Unity, we passed the yellow road sign with a horse and buggy on it. Since the Amish live right next to a small town, this was one of the few things that signaled we were near their homes.

We would have stayed with Christina, but her house was too full of guests who came for the wedding. Instead, we were going to stay at Esther's house.

Since I did not remember Esther's address or how to get there, we went to Christina's house first so I could get the address to put in my GPS.

As we drove down a lane in the Amish community, there were several Amish children playing outside. It was so good to be back. It had been about eight months since my last visit, and I sure had missed it. There is something very peaceful about this Amish community, something captivating, almost like time stands still there. It's almost like going back in time.

We drove beyond the community store and Christina's brother Caleb's house, and further down the lane until we reached Christina's house.

Hailey was surprised to see huge solar panels on the front porch. As I parked my car, I noticed an Amish man watching us from the barn doorway. We walked to the house and up the steps, and I knocked. Once, twice, three times. I peeked in the window and saw several Amish girls mopping the floor.

"They must be getting ready for the wedding," I said.

"They probably don't hear you knocking," Hailey said. "Maybe you should knock harder."

Just then the Amish man came up the steps. It was Christina's father-in-law, Isaac, but I had not recognized him from a distance.

"Hi, I'm a friend of Christina's. Is she here?" I asked him.

"Oh, she is at Caleb's right now. If you want, you may wait inside for her." He opened the door for me. Caleb was Christina's brother.

"Well, I just was going to ask her what Esther's address was because I forgot. We are staying there tonight and they are expecting us. Do you know their address or their street?"

"Oh, yes, but I just can't think of it. It is near the intersection." He thought for a moment then he remembered and told me. "You may go see Christina at Caleb's house."

I told him we would, and Hailey and I walked back to my car. Isaac went inside, but then one of the girls came out and told us Christina had just come in through the back door, so we went back up the steps.

I watched my feet, trying not to step on my dress. When I reached the top, I looked up, and there was Christina.

She hugged me, and I said, "It's so great to see you again."

Seeing her was indeed a delight. She has such a friendly personality and warm smile. I introduced her to Hailey, and then we went inside.

There were so many girls inside the house cooking and cleaning. One lady introduced herself as Jolene's aunt from Pennsylvania. She had come with her three nieces by train, which had been two hours late. We thought we had a long drive, but our drive took as long as their train was late— two hours.

(Below is a photo of a kerosene lamp and prayer kapp in Christina's bathroom. They actually don't use kerosene lanterns for safety reasons, so this might have been more of a decoration. They use battery-operated lights.)

I introduced Hailey to everyone, and several people thought she was my sister.

Christina's young daughter, Damaris, had grown much taller. I couldn't believe how much she'd changed in such a short time. I think she recognized me when she looked at me, but she mostly looked at us shyly from behind her mother's skirt. It was hard to believe that was the same little girl I had bonded with, who had cried when I left.

Isaac's wife came upstairs and hugged me. "How is life treating you?" she asked.

"Very well. It is so good to see everyone again." I was also excited to see Jolene's mom. Last time I saw her, she was sad because she thought she might not see me again.

All this time, I wondered what Hailey thought of everything. There was a lot going on, but she smiled at everyone and was talkative and friendly. It would be interesting later when I had a chance to speak with her privately and learn what she thought of it all.

Christina asked if we wanted to help with the wedding, and of course we said yes. An Amish girl named Liz was asked to go with us next door to pick up some dishes for the wedding. She was the one who had called me yesterday to let me know I would be sleeping at Esther's house.

Liz put on her boots and came with us into my car. On the way, I walked right into the clothesline, and we all laughed when it flung water on to me. It had been raining and had stopped right before we arrived. There were flowers everywhere, very different from when I had been there last October.

We cleared out the back seat for Liz, and I put our bags and my Bible in the trunk.

As we rolled out of the driveway, I addressed Liz. "Where are you from?"

"Smyrna."

"I want to drive Esther's family there to visit their aunt someday. Isn't Smyrna a much larger community than Unity?"

"Yes. And now there is another one starting near it," she said.

"So many people don't know about this community, or even that there are Amish communities in Maine. They think the only one is in Lancaster, and that's where everyone thought I was visiting."

Liz said, "There are communities all over the country that many people don't know about. Many of the wedding guests are visiting from communities in Ontario, Pennsylvania, Kentucky, and Tennessee."

"I didn't know they were in Canada, too," I said.

"There are really a lot more than many people know about."

Hailey said, "I think I saw an Amish woman in Arundel. I wonder if there is a community there too."

Arundel was right near my house. It was something I'd have to look into.

We drove to Christina's neighbor's house first to get the dishes. On the way down her narrow lane, with a ditch on one side and a pond on the other, a buggy passed us. I pulled over, scared we would fall off the road and into the water. Liz was calm, and told me that there was enough room for both of us and, surprisingly, there was.

Liz went inside to look for the dishes, but they did not have the right ones. We went back to Christina's, and she told us to try asking her mother, Elizabeth.

Elizabeth's house was also full of people. There were two cars there with people dressed in modern clothes. I wondered if we would look silly to them in our long dresses, but we wanted to blend in with the Amish as much as possible.

I shrugged it off. I didn't know what people would be wearing tomorrow, and they would probably just assume we followed a religion similar to Amish anyway, not that we were *Englishers* trying to blend in with the Amish.

When we got inside, Elizabeth found me and I introduced her to Hailey, then we tried to figure out what would fit in my car. There were two large coolers, a bag of dishes, and a propane tank. We decided to take it all with us. Hailey helped us carry the things out to my car. We somehow fit it all in, along with our bags, and we went to the schoolhouse. We brought everything into the basement and went upstairs.

Liz explained they had moved the schoolroom divider aside for the wedding, so it was all open and connected to the room where church services were held. The chairs were set up in a circular shape so they all faced a pulpit in the middle of the room.

"That is where the couple will be married," Liz said, motioning to the spot. She explained how the classroom usually looks like a classroom with decorations, posters, and students' artwork on the walls. Now, even though most of the decorations were temporarily taken down, the blackboards remained.

"After she gets married, Jolene will not be teaching anymore. Regina will start as a replacement temporarily," Liz said. "They are looking for a new teacher."

I asked, "Does the teacher have to be Amish?"

"Yes," Liz said.

"The students were so well-behaved when I taught here in October. If all classes were like that, I would be a teacher. But not all classes are so respectful. Right, Hailey?"

"Right. Some kids are really rude in my class at school, especially to the teacher. And some kids bully other kids."

"I can't imagine that happening here," Liz said.

We went back to Caleb's. As we drove down the main road, cars sped on by. Some of the boys had been playing a volleyball game earlier, but Liz said they had been rained out.

I dropped Liz off at Caleb's at her request, and Hailey and I went to Esther's.

"Do you think they'll like me? What if they think I'm weird because I'm different from them?" Hailey asked, fidgeting in her seat.

"Of course, they will love you! I'm an outsider, and they all like me. They won't think you're weird at all. They might ask you a lot of questions though. They'll just want to get to know you."

"I feel silly wearing this dress." Hailey poked at her skirt. "I'm not used to wearing clothes like this."

"You don't have to wear it if you don't want to. I only do it to blend in. I want to experience the Amish way of life as much as I can, and this helps me feel a bit closer to them somehow. I know I'm not actually Amish, but when I stayed here for a week, I really felt like I was Amish for a week," I explained. "It was life-changing."

"Well, I guess I'll wear it then. I don't really want to wear jeans if no one else is."

I laughed. "Well, don't feel like you have to do either. It's all up to you. They won't care if you wear jeans."

I finally found Esther's house, and we passed Timothy, one of her children, in his buggy. We realized he had been the one we passed earlier at Christina's neighbor's house. I parked the car while one of the children was waiting at the door, telling us to come on in.

The front room had a cement floor and contained an old-fashioned Maytag washer, a wood stove, a clothesline, and about thirteen pairs of black shoes lined up against the wall in sizes ranging from very small to large.

Esther came out and shook our hands, and we went inside. Maria and Ella Ruth came right up to us and greeted us, and I introduced Hailey to everyone. She looked shy, but once everyone greeted her so warmly, she became more talkative.

There was a big clothing rack where clothes were drying by the woodstove while they made potato and egg salad.

Besides Esther and Maria, there was only one other woman in the kitchen who looked to be in her mid-twenties.

"Hi, I'm Betty. I'm also here for the wedding," she said.

"Hi, I'm Ashley. Nice to meet you." I looked around. "Where is everyone else? At school?"

"No, school is out for the summer. The others are out or taking naps. They woke up very early this morning," Esther said.

"What can we do to help?" I asked.

Maria gave us some celery to cut up. Betty was using a mashing machine for the potatoes. She put boiled potatoes in it and it mashed them like a hand masher would, except it was much faster. It was, of course, not run by electricity, but with a hand-operated handle.

They asked me about work and what I'd been doing, and I told them about the book I had written about my stay in Unity.

"I didn't bring enough copies, so I will mail one for you and one for Elizabeth."

"What is it called?" Esther asked.

"Ashley's Amish Adventures." (I recently changed the book title, but originally, this was the title.)

They laughed and smiled. "That's a great name."

Lily came downstairs from her nap, her hair loose and hanging to her knees. Since no men were around, I guess she didn't feel the need to cover it. I introduced her to Hailey, and I told her she and Hailey were both twelve years old.

When no one was listening, Hailey whispered to me, "Their hair is so long! Should I put mine up like theirs?"

I said, "No. It's okay. They don't expect us to do everything like them."

One of the other girls also had her hair down because it had been washed and now was air-drying. There were so many people in their house that they had to take showers in the middle of the day.

After we cut all the celery, Ella Ruth took us to our room. It was a different one than last time. They had other visitors staying in the guest room where I had previously stayed. So this time we had Ella Ruth's room to ourselves.

(Below is a picture of one of the girl's closets. As you can see, this girl kept her prayer kapp on a container to keep its shape. There are lotions, perfume, and a mirror on the bureau, which may surprise some people. They do use products like this because they do not change one's appearance. However, they do not wear makeup.)

(Below is a photo of one of the other bedrooms.)

"Where will you sleep?" I asked her.

"With my sisters in their room." She motioned to the room across the hall.

"Thanks so much for letting us use your room."

She was so gracious. "You're welcome. We're really glad to have you here."

We went out to the car to get our bags. Irvin asked me to move the car later because there were more guests coming. While I backed up, I made sure no kids, dogs, or cats were behind me.

(Below is a photo of the clothesline behind Esther's house.)

Hailey said as I backed up the car in the driveway, "The little ones are watching us from the porch."

I looked, and sure enough there were some curious children watching us who had just awakened from their nap.

We brought our bags up to our room. On the wall were pictures of people. There were calendars, cards, letters, and scrapbook pages. Though they are not allowed to be in pictures themselves, I had not realized until then that they were not against having pictures of other people.

It took me an hour to write down everything that had happened that day so I wouldn't forget it. Once I finished, we went downstairs to finish helping with dinner. There sure were a lot of people to cook for. The kitchen was very hot with the wood stove, and I wondered how hot it got in the summer.

As we cooked, I noticed how well Hailey was doing. This was a totally different environment for her, yet she was quickly adjusting and making new friends.

As we mixed the almost finished potato and egg salad, Maria said, "There will be one hundred fifty people eating at Caleb's house tonight, and there will be three hundred guests tomorrow at the wedding. That is a lot of people to cook for!"

Instead of getting a caterer, several Amish families pitched in to make food for all the guests, which is typical of many Amish weddings.

I asked, "How will they all fit in the church? And who will cook all that food?"

Maria said, "It will be tight, but they will fit. The service will be from 9:00 to 12:00."

"I have to leave early for work around 11:45," I told them. "It's a long drive and I have to be at work by 2:00." I was disappointed that I would not be able to stay a while after the wedding.

"Well, at least you will get to see the marriage, but you will miss the lunch after," Ella Ruth said. "Too bad you have to leave early."

They asked us what types of dances we learned this year at our dance studio. I told them about the lyrical duet I had taught to Hailey and her sister.

In October, I had taught dance in the Amish schoolhouse, mostly hip hop with a warmup. The children in the schoolhouse had all learned the moves so quickly, even though they had not even known what a jumping jack was.

Betty asked to see one of the moves I had shown them, so I showed her some hip hop dance steps. She laughed and smiled. "Wow!" she said, as if she'd never seen dancing before.

Lily and I reminisced about the paper frogs we had made when I had last been there, and we laughed about the games we had played—the clothespin game and Evolution, the drawing game.

"Let's play Evolution tonight after dinner," Lily said.

"We could play Evolution and the clothespin game at the same time," I suggested.

"That would be fun!" Lily said.

Ella Ruth and Maria said they were going to go pick strawberries outside.

"Do you need help?" I asked.

"You might get wet," was Ella Ruth's response. "The bushes are wet from the rain."

I shrugged it off, saying we had changes of clothes. We, along with several of the other girls, went outside.

We went out into the strawberry patch, which was in the garden, and searched through the wet leaves for red strawberries. I kept picking the green ones by accident because they were red on the top.

Betty asked me, "Have you ever picked strawberries before?"

"Only at the pick-your-own strawberry places where you have to pay."

Ella Ruth said, "This is the first year we are growing strawberries. We used to have to pay to pick them, too."

One of the girls hollered, "I think I just saw a snake!"

A few of the girls shrieked in response.

I said, "I'd rather see a snake than a spider. Snakes don't scare me."

"I'd rather see a spider. I don't like snakes," Betty said. "I caught a few at my house, but still there was one more."

"Where are you from?" I asked.

"Smyrna."

"Do you know Liz? She's from there too."

"Yes! She is my neighbor. I've known her a long time."

I then realized that if I looked closely enough, there were many spiders in the plants. I ignored it, even though I am scared of spiders, and kept on picking. Soon we had three buckets full of strawberries. Seth joined us, but he was too young to help. He just ate the strawberries.

Laura said, "That strawberry looks like it could slide down my throat." We laughed as she ate it.

We moved up and down the rows, tossing berries into the bucket. Then the mosquitoes came out, but they weren't too bad.

"Do you have a garden, Ashley?" Betty asked me.

"We do. Well, it's my mother's garden. I'm not any good with plants. It's almost as big as Caleb's, and we are going to plant it soon, but we have never grown strawberries."

We heard some rustling in the strawberry bushes and looked over at Seth, Esther's two-year-old son, and laughed at his red-stained face and hands. He was even eating the green strawberries.

Esther came outside and said we were invited to go to the big dinner at Caleb's at six. I asked Hailey what she thought, and we decided we'd go later. Then Esther and Irvin left early because they were going to be serving food.

I really wanted to meet other people from other communities, so I hoped to still go later on that night.

We finished picking, and by then the hems on our dresses were wet from the strawberry plants. Everyone other than Hailey and I had been barefoot. I told Hailey I had an extra dress for her, and we changed into dry clothes.

Some strawberries were moldy and some had white tips. Ella Ruth said she'd just cut the tips off and throw out the moldy ones. We would have the good ones for dessert with dinner and the rest with breakfast.

We went inside to clean them. Ella Ruth rinsed them, cut them up and put them in a bowl like an expert.

We sat at the table and talked for a little while, and then I asked if we could show Hailey the barn. So Hailey, Maria, Debra, Naomi, Seth, and I set out for the barn.

The barn is not the red, rustic image that may come to your mind, but the inside looks like any other barn, complete with loads of hay and animals.

(The barn is pictured below.)

(Below is a photo of Esther and Irvin's house and bike shop.)

I noticed the empty space where the goats used to be. "Where are all the goats?"

"They are outside in the pasture during the day," Maria said.

They have nine kittens and two cats, and there was a mother cat with one kitten in the fenced-in area. Maria picked up the kitten and Hailey held it.

The other cats were high up on a rafter, and there was a ladder on the wall leading up to them. Debra and Seth climbed up, and I was scared they or the kittens would fall the whole time. But they climbed like they knew exactly what they were doing, and no one fell.

The little kittens looked over the edge of the rafter. When Seth ran across the boards, they shook, and I thought one of the kittens would fall off, but they didn't. As I looked up, I realized there were literally dozens of big spiders all over the ceiling with sprawling webs. I have never seen so many spiders in one place. I was afraid one would fall on my head.

Naomi observed me looking at them. She asked me, "Do you like spiders?"

"No!" I tried not to look up again. "I'm scared of them."

They showed Hailey the rest of the animals. There were several huge black pigs, a cow, and a horse. We went out of the barn and their dog, a Corgi, came up to us.

"What's his name? Zeke? Zack?" I couldn't quite remember what it was from last time.

"It's Zeb! You were close," Maria said.

Then a little beagle puppy came barreling around the corner, half the size of Zeb. She jumped on Seth, who laughed and ran away. Then the little dog jumped on Zeb, trying to instigate a playful fight. Zeb was completely unamused.

The smaller dog sniffed us all and energetically ran around. Maria said that her name was Zoe. Zoe grabbed a stick, ran around with it, then dropped it. I threw it, and while Zeb starting barking, Zoe didn't even see it.

We went into the bike shop and talked about the last time I was there. We had to sweep the whole building...and it was quite big. Maria said that her brothers get old bikes and fix them up to sell, and they sell parts. Her dad makes windmills and maple syrup to sell. I almost brought them maple syrup as a gift, and I was so glad I didn't now!

Debra and Seth started playing around, and Hailey asked them how old they are. Seth said he was now three and Debra said she was five. They both had had birthdays since I was there last.

I asked Maria, "Do you celebrate birthdays?"

She said, "Well, we have cake, but it's not that big of a deal."

I said, "Do you celebrate Christmas?"

She said, "No, but some of the families celebrate Thanksgiving. In school we usually get one day off for Thanksgiving."

We looked at the clock and realized it was 6:00 p.m.

I said, "It's too late to go to Caleb's. We'll get there when everyone is eating."

Hailey said, "Can we just stay here then?"

"You are welcome to stay," Maria offered. "We'd love to have you here for dinner."

So we went inside and told Ella Ruth we were staying. All the boys and their friends came in. There were five or six of them. The table was set, and we all sat down for dinner. Hailey and I sat at the end.

One of the older boys said, "Let's bow our heads and see who will ask the blessing." Then another boy prayed. I was surprised at this, because usually they either pray silently or the father prays, but their dad was not there. We had beef stew and the potato salad with bread and jam and the strawberries.

After dinner, everyone sang a song, but Hailey and I didn't know the words. We cleared the table and did dishes while playing the clothespin game.

"This is going to take forever without a dishwasher," Hailey whispered.

"It'll be fun. We'll be done before you know it," I told her.

We had played this game last time I visited. In the game, everyone received five clothespins. A word was chosen that was not allowed to be spoken during the game. Whoever said it had to give up a clothespin to the person who caught them saying the certain word. Whoever had the most clothespins at the end of the game won. It is trickier than it sounds.

Naomi and Rosanna said, "Let's do the word 'what' like last time." So we chose that.

"What can we do to help?" I asked, and, of course, one of the girls took one of my clothespins. I hadn't even meant to say "what." It is such a common word, I had said it without thinking.

We helped Betty wash the dishes. I rinsed and Lily and Hailey dried. I helped them dry when their dishes piled up, then my dishes piled up.

Hailey said, "Ashley?"

"What?" I replied before thinking.

"You said it!" She took one of my clothespins.

Lily told a story and Betty said, "She did what?"

Hailey said something to me quietly in Spanish and I said without thinking, "What?" Each time we laughed harder and harder at each other's gullibility.

After everything was put away, we played Evolution, which is like Pictionary, except the pictures are changed by the players throughout the game. One person would write a word, then the next person would draw it, then the next person would write down what they thought it was, then the next person would draw that word, and so on.

I wrote down "windmill," but that didn't really end up evolving. Then I wrote "us picking strawberries" on my card and by the time it had been passed around the table so everyone could try drawing it, it had turned into someone picking flowers and cherries.

The boys passed around hymn books and started singing while we continued to play. I wrote "us playing evolution" on my card, and it turned into the boys singing at the table.

After a few more rounds of laughter we stopped playing because we were too loud and were interrupting the boys, so we joined in their singing. We sang from a song book that had been written by a family after losing several members in an accident. I didn't think they were allowed to sing songs from books that were not in the *Ausbund*, the Amish hymnal.

I asked, "So, is this separate from the *Ausbund*?"

"Yes. We sing the *Ausbund* in church," Lily said. "Usually we are not allowed to sing songs outside the *Ausbund*, but we are allowed to sing this song because an Amish family wrote it, and it has become accepted."

We sang a few songs, then Hailey and I brushed our teeth because we knew the bathrooms would be full later. Then Irvin, Esther, Maria, and more guests arrived from Caleb's house.

Esther asked, "Why didn't you come to Caleb's house?"

"We lost track of time because we were having so much fun here!"

We drew pictures, and I made Seth more paper frogs. The younger children drew pictures. I drew a profile of Rosanna, and it ended up looking a lot like her.

Debra played a silly game with me, laughing while she tried to keep my hands around my water bottle and I tried to move my hands away.

I asked the girls how to say several words and phrases in German. I guessed many of them correctly.

"Who wants to learn a word game?" I said, and they all wanted to learn. "Can you say 'toy boat' very quickly five times in a row?" They tried it over and over, but no one could do it. We laughed until our sides hurt.

I showed them how to do a trick with their fingers. When Rosanna learned how to do it correctly, Hailey said, "High five!" and held her hand up. Rosanna looked at her in confusion.

"You don't know how to high five?" Hailey asked.

Rosanna shook her head.

"Well, then," Hailey said. "I'm going to teach you how."

After, we cleaned up the big mess of cut up paper and drawings from Evolution, and then it was time for bed. Irvin gave us a battery-operated light, and we went upstairs. The younger children came in our room and said, "Shlafenzeit," which means 'goodnight.' It is almost the same as how I learned it in German in high school. Maria led the children to their rooms.

"So, what do you think so far, Hailey?" I asked as we got into bed.

"Everyone is really nice. It sure is different here. I don't know how they live without a dishwasher or microwave or TV. They all seem happy though. It was nice to play games and get to know everyone."

"See? I told you that everyone would love you and you'd have fun."

At 10:30 p.m., someone down the hall began singing, "Great is Thy Faithfulness." The clock on our wall played "Amazing Grace" every hour. I took out the batteries because I am such a light sleeper, and the ticking kept me awake.

I did not sleep much that night. I was not used to sharing a bed, and I woke up several times thinking it was morning. Around 5:00 a.m., the birds were very loud and the window was open, but I was too afraid to move and possibly wake up Hailey to close it.

It seemed as though I had just fallen asleep when I heard commotion downstairs, and it was time to get up. I waited in the hallway for about ten minutes for the bathroom to brush my teeth, waiting around the corner because anytime one of the boys or men would see me in the hallway they would duck behind the door.

I wondered why they did that, and I realized it was probably because they didn't want to see me still in my pajamas. So I stayed hidden, peeking around the corner every time I heard a noise. I missed the bathroom three times. Finally, the door opened and I dashed down the hallway and got in before anyone else could.

Hailey and I brought our bags downstairs and everyone else was sitting down. The older girls had already left to serve the food and set up at the church.

At the table was a married couple who had also stayed there overnight. I had no idea where Esther fit everyone, but apparently her family was used to having several guests.

Right before prayer, the puppy and the cat got into a loud spat outside on the porch and made such funny noises that everyone laughed. We prayed right afterward, and it was all Hailey and I could do to not break the silence with our giggles.

Irvin lead the silent prayer. I was glad I had explained this to Hailey earlier, so she knew to expect it.

The food was passed around. It was a few kinds of cereal in tall, plastic containers and the strawberries we had picked last night. There was also apple crisp and cookies. They really do have dessert at every meal.

I sat next to Naomi. She offered me cereal and asked what time I was leaving, and I was regretful as I explained I had to leave right after the ceremony. Soon the spoons were scraping bowls as everyone finished their cereal.

Irvin said, "Let's sing our after-meal hymn," and led the doxology.

I whispered to Hailey, "We actually know this one." We usually didn't know the songs they sing, but this was a song that we both grew up singing in church.

Right after singing, Irvin glanced at the clock. "We have time to pray."

I thought we were going to kneel at our chairs as usual, but everyone stood and made their way to the living room.

Hailey whispered, "What are we doing?"

"I think we are doing devotionals."

Everyone sat in the living room, and we sat on the stairs. Irvin read the passage in Revelation 19 about the marriage supper of the lamb. He talked about how we must be ready at all times for the day Jesus will return. Then one of the other men led us in prayer which was entirely in German. I recognized many words, especially in the Lord's Prayer at the end.

We cleared the dishes and helped wash them. A woman who stayed overnight, whose name I cannot remember, asked me where I was from and asked if Hailey and I were sisters or friends.

"We are friends, and we live a half hour away from each other. We dance together at our dance studio."

The woman said she and her husband came from Pennsylvania. She knew Liz and Betty, who are also from there.

I asked, "How did Abner get to know so many people in Pennsylvania?"

She said, "He traveled a lot, though he grew up here. I think he also had some relatives in Pennsylvania. Jolene and Abner both live here, even though Jolene is originally from Kentucky. They are friends with everyone here, but many guests will be coming from out of state."

"Wow. I can't wait to meet more people," I said, excited to meet Amish from other states.

We put all the dishes away and carried our bags to the car. On the way out the door, I realized they had a regular washing machine, which could not have worked because they did not have electricity. I wondered why, but I never got the chance to ask.

Esther came outside. "Did the girls show you the chicks yet?"

"No, we totally forgot yesterday. We were too busy seeing the barn animals," Hailey said.

She brought us into the greenhouse, saying it was warm in there for them. And it sure was. There were two big boxes full of chickens. One had red chickens, and one had chickens called black giants. They were so fluffy and funny, climbing over each other and peeping. She also had regular chickens in another box that were losing the fluffy part of their feathers because they were growing older.

She said, "The black and red ones are for eggs, while the regular ones are for eating, and they aren't as cute. We made the boxes for them out of several smaller boxes and stapled them together."

The dog, Zoe, scampered around, chewing on feathers. I heard fluttering wings and pointed out that a butterfly was stuck in the corner.

Esther said, "This greenhouse is a butterfly trap. This is where Maria gets her butterfly collection."

I asked her if that was on purpose, and she explained, "We have to leave the doors open so it's not too hot for the chicks and the butterflies just get stuck in here. Lots of bugs do."

I asked Esther, "Do you think people will be at the church by now?"

"Yes. The older girls already left. Maybe they could use some help, or you could go early and get a good seat."

"Okay, we will go there now. Do you want me to take any of your girls with me?"

A few of the girls liked this idea and asked her if they could, but she told them it was too early and they might get bored. So I told them we'd see them there later.

We were about to go out the door when Esther said, "Would you have time to write in my guest book?"

I had not done so last time I was there. "Sure. Where is it?"

Esther asked Naomi to show us, and she brought us back into the living room to a roll-top desk. She pulled out a white guest book. We found a pen and I wrote the date, my name, and a brief note. *It was good to see you all again. Lots of fun—thanks so much!* Then Hailey wrote something, too.

We went outside, and the two dogs were wagging around. We played with them for a little while. The little beagle liked to bite, but she only had puppy teeth so it didn't hurt. She just wanted to play. Then the cat came over, and when we put our bags in the trunk, she jumped inside the trunk.

After we finally got her out and got in the car, the beagle tried to climb in the backseat. After I got her to back away, I was scared I would hit one of the many animals while backing up. I had Hailey stand outside to make sure I didn't run them over.

On the way to the church, Hailey looked at the other houses. "So, do other people who are not Amish live with or stay with Amish people?"

I thought she meant people like me who visit and live in their homes so I said, "I don't know. I might be one of the few."

She said, "No. I meant these non-Amish families who have houses right next to them."

"Oh, yes. They live next to non-Amish people. A lot of people think they have their own separate community, like in the movies. But many Amish, like the Amish here, live next to other people and gas stations and pizza restaurants. Lots of people think the Amish only live in Lancaster, but they are all over the place, as Liz said. Wherever there is enough farm land and enough people for a church, you may find Amish families scattered across the country. However, I think we are one of only a few *Englishers* who have lived with them in their homes."

On the short ride to the church, we passed several buggies and groups of Amish people walking down the road mixed with *Englishers* in modern clothes.

Hailey asked, "Can I take a picture?"

"They don't like to be in pictures. You probably shouldn't."

There were so many of them coming from all directions. This wedding would be big. We arrived, and it was strange to me to see all the cars in the lot mixed in with the buggies. When I had been here last time,

144

we had the only car in the whole parking lot, but today I was not the only non-Amish guest. I parked near the exit so I could leave quickly for work.

(Below is a somewhat blurry photo of a horse and buggy I took from inside my car.)

Two school buses came in packed with Amish people. One Amish young man my age looked right at me for more than a few seconds, and I quickly looked away out of respect, surprised. Most of the Amish boys and men had not acknowledged me, talked to me, or even looked at me at all. I did not know if it was out of shyness or if they were raised that way.

Hailey called her mom on my cell phone. She told her how the Amish have toilets, plastic dishes, and battery-operated flashlights. She said it was different than she had thought it would be. She was having fun, and she was writing about it, too.

As Hailey was on the phone, I watched everyone outside. From trails in the woods came more Amish people and more came down the lane. This certainly was a big occasion.

I got a few strange looks as I walked inside with my car keys while wearing old-fashioned clothes. I wondered what they thought of me, but I wasn't as self-conscious as I was when I first came here.

When we went inside, I recognized Sharon and Regina, and I introduced Hailey to them.

Sharon said, "Ashley, we have a new baby girl in our family, a three-week-old. I will try to find her to show her to you." But there were so many people around, I doubted I'd get to see her.

I was going to introduce Hailey to more people, but I wanted good seats. So, we sat down in the back of the room where there were chairs instead of backless benches. Edward came up to us and told us the translator would be sitting on the opposite end of the church, so he led us to different seats so we could hear better.

I had no idea there would even be a translator. I was prepared to listen to three hours of German and trying to translate it myself.

The church is made up of three rooms. The first floor is a hall where the after-church luncheons are served. The floor is cement, and there is a wood stove and propane burner. Upstairs is divided into two parts.

As Liz had explained to us when we had dropped off the dishes yesterday, one half is the school room and the other half is the room where church is held. The wall between the two rooms had been removed.

All the chairs faced the center where the two rooms met. That was where the speaker would stand. At the end of the service, that was where Jolene and Abner would stand as they were married.

In the school room where the walls and ceiling met, there was still a border of numbers and letters. Book shelves still stood, holding encyclopedias and textbooks. The chalkboard and dry erase board remained on the walls, but everything else that was school-related had been temporarily moved out. However, there were no decorations or finery. The bride and groom wore clothes that looked just like clothes they usually wore, and they did not at all stand out from the guests.

After we sat down, I realized I had left Jolene and Abner's gift in the car. While Hailey stayed at our seats, I found Christina and asked her where I should put it, and she showed me the spot in the room where others had left gifts. These gifts were nothing like the elaborately wrapped you'd see at most weddings. These had simple wrappings such as bags, baskets, or boxes rather than colorful wrapping paper, bows, or gift bags. I don't know what type of gift were inside, but I imagine they were simple, practical, or homemade.

I went to get it in the car, and when I returned, I left it with the others. It was a brown paper bag with maple syrup, some homemade canned foods my mother had made, and a signed copy of the earliest version of this book.

I was going to say goodbye to Christina, but she was busy helping people and talking to people. I figured I would ask Esther to say goodbye to her for me later.

I returned to my seat next to Hailey. By now the room was packed, and I was glad we had saved our seats in advance. There were several girls sitting next to us who were my age. I introduced myself, and the two who were sitting next to us told us their names—Loulie and Hope. I don't know what religion they were, and I didn't know how to ask. The girl sitting next to me wore a dress similar to an Amish dress, but it had beads on it, so I knew it was not. She also had painted toes and sandals, two things also against the Amish custom. Instead of *kapps*, they wore handkerchiefs on their heads. I'd have to ask someone about them later when it wouldn't seem rude.

We each got a pamphlet with songs from the *Ausbund.*

Loulie whispered to her friend, "This is all in German."

"The English part is written right below the German words," I pointed out. "I can sing the English part with you if you want. Do you know German?"

"No, we don't."

"I learned some in high school. Where are you from?"

"Tennessee. We are distant relatives of Abner." He really did have family from all over.

"Is this really going to be three hours long?" Hayley whispered. "That's such a long time."

"Yes, it'll be three hours. This is an experience not many people get to see who aren't Amish though. I think you'll like it more than you think," I whispered back. Yes, it was a long time, but many non-Amish people would love to attend an Amish wedding, so we should be grateful for the opportunity, even if we were about to sit on backless benches for three hours.

Everyone stopped talking as the wedding started at five of nine. They sure were on time. We sang the German hymns for the first fifty minutes.

I could tell one of the girls next to me was getting fidgety. It was a long time to sing songs you didn't understand, and the songs were very slow. And since we did not understand the words, it seemed a lot longer than fifty minutes. Hailey was completely patient throughout the entire service, although we both got a little antsy and anxious for it to be over so we could move around.

Then a man gave a message in German. Right before the man started to speak, another man came into the room and sat with us in the non-Amish section. He then began speaking in a loud voice, "Brothers and sisters, we are gathered here today to celebrate the marriage of this young man and woman…"

Why is he talking like that? What is he trying to do, talk over the minister and disrupt the wedding?

I wasn't the only one who thought that, because he received several strange looks from other people sitting with us. I then realized he was the translator Edward had mentioned. I have never experienced sitting next to a translator before, except for when Christina had translated the church service for me in October. But she had been very quiet, and this man was speaking loud so our half of the room could hear him. It was strange to hear them both speaking at once, especially since I knew bits of what the man was saying in German.

Every now and then the translator would pause and say, "I didn't get that…. Anyway…" and continue on. The man speaking in German was across the room so sometimes the translator didn't hear him. After the man speaking in German was done, the translator slipped out as quickly as he had slipped in. I wondered why he did not stay. Perhaps he had done his job and saw no reason to stay if he did not personally know the bride or groom.

Abner's brother Caleb spoke next. He spoke in English, and I was grateful to understand. He talked about when Abner was little and the responsibility of the man being the leader of the household. He said a good marriage takes two good forgivers. I liked that point. He spoke of when their father had died, and I saw Caleb and Abner's mother Elizabeth from across the room shedding a few tears. I prayed for God to comfort her.

Next to speak was the bishop. As he spoke into the third hour, I felt very fortunate to have a chair with a backing. Many people sat on not so comfortable benches for the three hours. The group of boys who sat on benches across from us put their elbows on their knees and their chins on their knuckles, looking like they would much rather be doing something else. But everyone was patient throughout the long service. I suppose they must be used to it because their regular church services are about two-and-a-half hours long.

The actual vows and marriage ceremony took about five minutes out of the entire service. The bishop called the bride and groom forward and asked them vows similar to the ones I have heard at other weddings, but they were worded a little differently. At the end, the bishop joined their hands together. He said that a three-cord strand is not easily broken. The three-cord strand represents the husband, the wife, and God. Instead of saying "I do" in response to the vows, they simply said, "Yes." Jolene was so calm, I was impressed. I hoped to be that calm on my wedding day.

Someone's phone went off loudly during the vows. It was rather jarring, and the man had to quickly leave the room. If that had been my phone, I would have been mortified. I double checked my phone, making sure it was on silent.

When the vows were complete, the bride and groom did not kiss. The bishop announced that they were married, and then another speaker began closing the ceremony. That must have signaled that the wedding was over, because several girls who were the servers left the room to get ready to serve lunch.

I glanced at the clock. The three-hour service was over, and it was time for us to leave if I wanted to be at work on time and have Hailey home in time.

On our way out the door, I found Esther downstairs. I told her we were leaving, and I hugged her, thanking her for letting us stay at her house. She said we would have to plan a time that was not so busy so we could just visit and spend time with each other. She wrote down their address for me so I could mail her a book and some letters.

"Please tell the others I said goodbye. We have to go right now, and everyone is upstairs."

"I will try," Esther replied.

I said goodbye to some of the other girls who were downstairs, and we went out to my car. As we drove home, we talked about our time in Unity and what Hailey thought of it. I was so happy to have been able to share such an experience with her. It was not what she thought it was going to be like, but better. She loved going and meeting everyone and learning about them. It certainly is hard to know what to expect the first time you go.

The next day, I heard from her mother about how Hailey was full of stories. She was so excited to tell her family about all she had learned. It is so great to see a young girl, only twelve, who embraces learning and steps out of her comfort zone. She was shy at first, but she chose to do the hard thing and reach out and meet new people of a totally different background.

I was nervous too, the first time I had gone, wondering what they would think of me—an outsider living in their community. But I soon realized how welcoming they are, and how they are in so many ways just like us. We all have something in common. There is always a way to connect with someone. Whether it is washing the dishes with them, picking strawberries, teaching them how to dance, or making paper frogs. There is always something you can do to relate to someone.

Update: December 9th, 2019

Staying with the Amish changed my life forever. Not only did it change my outlook on life and show me what is most important, but it catapulted my author career into success.

Because of them, I was able to learn so much about them and use my experiences with them to write my novels. Now I am a full-time Amish-fiction author, making a full-time income from my novels. If it wasn't for these families who let me stay with them, even though I was a total stranger, I don't know if my books would have been successful.

My family owes my Amish friends so much more than they will ever know. I plan on visiting them again soon to take new photographs to add to this book, and I'm so excited to see my friends again who I have not seen in over six years. I might even bring my young daughter and write about the experience to add to this book.

I love this group of people who are so misunderstood and admired—the Amish.

BONUS CONTENT

Returning to Unity for a Visit with my Fiancé

April 6th, 2013

A lot has happened since I stayed with the Amish. I got engaged to a man named David Emma (who is now my husband). David regularly plays bass in different shows and musicals. On April 6, 2013, David played in the Rick Charette concert in Brewer, Maine. Rick Charette is a New England celebrity who has been singing silly, well-known children's songs for over thirty years. David was the bass player in Rick Charette's band, the Bubble Gum Band. After the concert, I realized that Unity was somewhat near Brewer, where we were.

"We should go visit Unity! Then you could meet everyone!" Excitement filled me at the thought of returning and seeing my friends.

"Okay, call them and ask if we can stop by," David said.

I called Christina's husband, Edward, since he has a business phone, and he invited us over for dinner.

We got a little lost because I could not remember any of their addresses, then we finally found it. First, we went to Esther and Irvin's house. We pulled up, knowing they were not expecting us. I didn't have their phone number, and I had not thought to ask Edward for it.

I threw my hands up. "Oh no! I'm wearing jeans."

"What do you mean? What did you wear last time?" David said, confused.

"I wore long dresses last time! I wanted the full experience. I didn't want to stand out, and I wanted to be respectful."

"I think they won't care if you wear what you usually wear," he assured me, and I knew he was right.

Irvin was in the front yard and came right up to us. He shook my hand and admitted he could not remember my name, but I reminded him and introduced David. I was relieved he recognized me. I explained how we were in the area and wanted to stop in and say hi.

"Are the others here?" I asked, and Irvin led us inside.

"Yes, they are." He walked inside as we took off our shoes and said, "Esther, look who is here!"

Esther saw me and hugged me, and I greeted all of the girls and introduced David to everyone. They offered us seats, and we sat and talked with them for a while.

Irvin asked David what he did for work, as did all three of the men of the families we visited that day. David told them about the sign company his father owns in Portland, where David works with his brother. They asked many questions about what signs they do and how the signs were made, and David explained how he made vinyl van wraps, big signs, light up signs, wraps for guitars, and foam letter signs. I even had a picture on my phone to show them.

All three of the families also asked David about his family, and David told them about his grandparents, who are Mennonite, and how we stayed with them for a week during Christmas. David also talked about his siblings and his mom's upbringing as a Mennonite.

I explained how David and I, along with our families and the Amish, do not have medical insurance. "It's just too expensive. But thankfully we have no debt because we did not go to college, so we have money saved up to put toward a house. Most people our age are in debt from college."

"Why didn't you go to college?" Esther asked David.

156

"My job did not require a college education. I knew I wanted to work for my dad," David told them. I think they could appreciate that. The Amish do not go to high school or college, and many (though not all) Amish boys work for their fathers and end up eventually taking over family businesses.

"Do you still have your chickens?" I asked the girls. There were several young girls surrounding Esther along with Seth, their youngest son.

"We do have all the red ones still, since they are for laying eggs, but we only have one black rooster left because they are for meat."

I understood what she meant by that statement. They had all been killed to eat. "Can we go see the ones you have in the barn?"

"Sure," Laura said, and we got dressed to go outside. I said goodbye to Irvin, Esther, Mariah, and Ella Ruth, knowing we would leave after. Laura, Seth, Naomi, and Debra brought us out to the huge barn. As soon as we opened the door, we flustered dozens of chickens and one rooster. The kids showed us the metal compartmentalized shelf that the chickens sat in to lay the eggs. They built a wide ladder out of tree limbs for the chickens and rooster to roost in. Laura filled the chickens' water bucket as one chicken pecked at the tip of my sneaker.

We explored the rest of the barn. Last time I had been there, there had been what seemed like hundreds of spiders on the ceiling, but the weather was cold now and I did not see any. However, the entire ceiling was still covered in layers of spider webs. It still creeped me out.

Laura noticed me looking up at the ceiling and asked me, "Do you like spiders?"

"Oh, no. I was looking for them because I'm scared of them." She had asked me that same question last time I had visited and my reply was the same. I really hate spiders!

We were shown two huge pigs, several goats, and two cats. David laughed at the goats, saying they made funny sounds.

The children ran to show us their huge greenhouse. Little Seth and Debra scampered down the hill, and David and I laughed at how adorable they were. Irvin's dog, a corgi named Zeb, ran out from where he had been sleeping and sniffed our shoes.

Their greenhouse was longer than their house, and the structure was covered in white plastic. David joked, "That house doesn't look green to me."

The children laughed. "Greenhouses aren't actually green!"

David told them he was only kidding as we passed by where we had picked strawberries in June. "Where did all the strawberry plants go?" I asked Laura.

"The strawberries will grow on their own when the weather gets warmer. They come back every year."

I was amazed at how some plants return annually without having to be planted again. All of this was good information for me in case I ever plant a garden in the future.

We stepped into the large greenhouse. The door caught in the wind behind us and slammed loudly. David and I jumped, but the children weren't fazed.

Naomi laughed and shrugged. "It does that all the time."

We looked at the expanse of the greenhouse. The grassy-looking floor was covered in parallel black tubes that resembled hoses. "We are growing tomatoes in here this year, and those black tubes are the irrigation system we use to water the plants. When we turn on the water, it sprays everywhere." Naomi showed us the tubes up close.

David and I were impressed. We had never seen anything quite like this before.

"Ready to see the other smaller greenhouse?" Laura asked.

The children brought us out of the large greenhouse and led us toward the smaller greenhouse where we had once shelled peanuts last time. As soon as we opened the door, we felt a wave of heat from the wood stove in the middle of the greenhouse.

"Wow, it's hot in here," we said.

David and I marveled at all the black trays containing rows of plants in their tiny compartments. We read all the labels that ranged from peppers to catnip to California W. I'm not sure what kind of plant that stood for.

There was a big box of dark soil, used to fill the trays of plants. I put my hand over the small wood stove and could not believe how hot it was. David noticed a spoon in the handle of the stove, and Laura told him they used that to turn the handle because the handle itself was too hot to touch.

As we exited the greenhouse, we saw Lily coming down the lane on her bicycle. I was so glad I would be able to see her before we left. I walked up to her, hoping she would recognize me, and she did.

"Hi, Ashley!" She waved and got off her bike.

"Hi! We just stopped by because we were in the area. I'm glad I got to see you!" I told her.

"It's great to see you. I actually just came from Caleb's house."

"David and I are going there later," I told her and introduced David to her as my fiancé.

I looked around and noticed two buggies in the driveway, wondering if they would mind if I took a picture. "Can I take pictures of your buggy?"

"Sure," Lily said, and I took a picture of the back of the buggy. When Lily realized she was in the shot, she ducked behind the bike shop.

(Above and below are Esther and Irvin's buggies.)

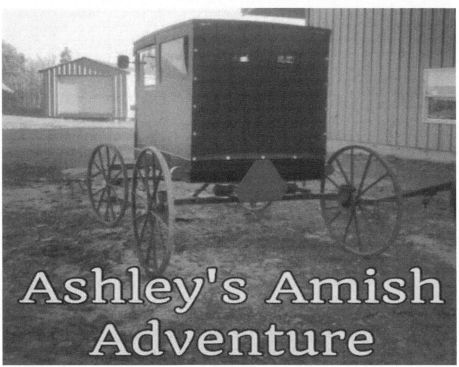

Ashley's Amish Adventure

"Irvin mentioned earlier that he did not recognize what was on the cover of my book so I'm taking new pictures to use for the cover." I snapped more pictures of the sides of the buggies to use as a new book cover that I would design myself. (This was back before I hired a graphic designer to make me professional-looking covers. The photo above is what I used for the older version of my cover.)

I turned to David, and he said we should probably leave so we'd have time to see Caleb and Christina. We thanked them for showing us around, said how great it was to see them, and left for Christina's house.

Where Christina lived, there was one shared driveway for her house, Caleb's house, and Caleb's store. Caleb's store is closest to the road, and as we turned into the drive way I showed David the store. It was closed, so we could not go in, but he at least got to see the outside of it. That was the first place I went when I first came to Unity. I remember asking the store clerk as many questions as I could about the Amish, until I realized he was also Amish, and I was so embarrassed. I laughed at how funny the memories were of when I first met the Amish of Unity. How little I knew about them back then.

We passed the store and approached Caleb's house next. We decided we would visit there last if we had time, and we drove on past to Christina's house, which was set very far back from the road. David tried to avoid the holes in the unpaved road as he drove, but my car bounced as we drove along. We pulled into Christina's driveway, and David laughed at how I still locked my car even though we were so far out in the country. It's just one of my habits.

We walked up the stairs to the main entrance of the three-story house, knocked on the door, and Christina opened it.

"Hi!" She smiled and hugged me. "It's so great to see you." Her young daughters, Damaris and Evangeline, stood by her side.

"Thanks. It's good to see you too. Thanks so much for letting us come by." I turned to the girls. "Wow! You are both so much taller than you were last time."

We went inside and Christina's husband Edward came in after us.

"This is my fiancé, David," I told him. "Our wedding is going to be in September. I was hoping you would be able to come, but maybe a two-hour car ride is too far to hire a driver for."

"I'm not sure, actually," she said. "I don't know what that would cost."

"I understand if that is too long of a trip to pay a driver for. Either way, I will send you an invitation!" I wasn't sure if they would come to an *Englisher's* wedding anyway. But I have thought a great many things about the Amish before I came here and have been completely wrong.

I had told David on the way here that Edward was rather reserved, but I suspected that was only because I'm an unmarried woman and he is a married man—the formal distance was likely only him being polite. He was probably just doing what he believed was proper, as most of the Amish boys and men did. Only a few ever spoke to me.

I had told David in the car that I thought Edward would converse with him much more because he is also a man, and I was right.

When David and Edward met, they hit it off right away. David told him we are going to buy land and build a house, and they started talking about buying and selling land and building houses.

"So what has been happening around here?" I asked Christina as they talked.

"Well, Jolene and Abner are expecting their first baby in a week or two," she told me as the two little girls ran around in the sunroom.

"Wow, that's great! It has been eight or nine months since I was last here." I laughed as Damaris and Evangeline spun in circles. "I can't believe how big Evangeline got since June. I think she was just a toddler then. So, who is teaching at the schoolhouse now?"

"Caleb's daughter Regina, and Ella Ruth."

"Oh, that's great that there are two of them. I just saw Ella Ruth, and we are going to see Caleb later if we have time."

"I think you will have time. Oh, and since Jolene and Abner bought and moved into my mother's house, my mother has moved in here with us," Christina said.

"Wonderful! So I get to see your mother tonight, too?"

Christina's mother's name was Elizabeth. I had been to her house before a few times. She had given me a jar of homemade soup to take home back in June that my family had loved.

Just then, Elizabeth came up the stairs, and she gave me a hug when she saw me. "What a surprise! How are you, Ashley?"

"I'm good. We were in the area and wanted to stop by. I wanted my fiancé to meet you all."

"Well, we are certainly glad you could come."

"Thank you. I'm glad we could too. What can I help with?"

Christina said I could peel eggs if I wanted to for egg salad for church the next day—the same dish I had helped Caleb's daughters make for church when I had first come here. Maybe it was a family recipe or a family favorite, but I didn't think to ask.

The girls were playing and the two men were talking, so I was glad for something to do.

I finished the task quickly, and Christina asked if David and I would like to see the barn before it got dark. Damaris wanted to take us, so she put on her coat and boots, and soon Evangeline wanted to join us. As they talked quietly with Christina, who helped them with their coats, they spoke Pennsylvania Dutch.

"Is that German?" David whispered in my ear. I barely noticed because I was used to hearing them speak their own language and I understood a good amount of it from the German I had learned in high school.

"Yes. Well, it is Pennsylvania Dutch," I whispered back. "They don't learn English until they go to school."

The girls finished getting bundled up and took us outside. They held hands as they slowly made their way down the stairs. The staircase had no railings, and as we progressed downward, there was nothing to hold on to. I offered my hand to Evangeline and she held it as she descended.

We reached the ground, and David had to duck out of the way of the clothesline that I had run into the last time I was here. We ran toward the barn, and two dogs came out to see us. One looked just like Irvin's corgi, Zeb.

"What's his name?" I asked Damaris.

"Her name is Freddy," she told me. She must have learned more English since I had last been here.

"So it's a boy?" David asked.

"No, she's a girl," Damaris corrected him.

David and I both looked at each other and laughed.

I had never seen the other dog before, a shaggy brown and white long-haired dog.

"That one's name is Gramps," Damaris said.

"Is that one a boy or a girl?" David asked.

Damaris thought a second, then shrugged her little shoulders. "I don't know." She giggled.

There was a large horse standing in the yard hitched up to a cart. David commented on how huge it was. I wanted to take a picture, but the girls were already going inside the barn. This barn looked more like the classic Amish barn one might imagine. It was completely made of wood, except for the metal roof. Inside it smelled of hay, dust, and animals. There was a cow, a large pig like Irvin's, and a pen of about thirty sheep and lambs.

We climbed up onto some boards and leaned over the railing. Several of the lambs sniffed our fingers and let out high pitched bleats. David and I laughed, saying they sounded like humans. The little lambs sounded like babies and the bigger ones sounded like adults.

"If I closed my eyes and didn't know where I was, I would think I was in a barn full of people making sheep noises! It is the only animal sound that actually sounds like how you spell it. Dog barks don't really sound like the word 'woof' and pig sounds don't really sound like the word 'oink,' but sheep noises really do sound like the word 'baa!'"

We laughed even harder at this realization, and one big sheep looked right at us and said, "Baaaaaa!"

We made our way out of the barn as Edward started feeding his chickens. Abner was walking down the driveway, and he approached us.

"Hi, I'm Abner." He shook David's hand. To me, he said, "Good to see you, Ashley."

"You, too! This is David, my fiancé. We are getting married in September. David, it was Abner and Jolene's wedding I went to back in June. Speaking of Jolene, I hear you are expecting a baby very soon."

"Yes, we are. We moved into Elizabeth's house."

"Christina told me. That's really great. I'm happy for you. I would love to come back sometime soon to visit. We are only stopping in for a bit today because we are in the area."

"All right. That sounds great. Well, it was nice to meet you," he said. We said goodbye and he drove the horse and cart down the lane.

Damaris ran up to us and said, "Evangeline is staying outside with *Dat*." (*Dat* means Dad. Some Amish also use the word Daed.)

We went into the house with Damaris. The table was set and the food was ready when we came back inside. Edward and Evangeline came in a moment later, and we all sat down at the table. Christina had David sit in Evangeline's usual seat, and the little girl asked who we were. She shyly looked at me then whispered something in Christina's ear, and Christina laughed. "She will be talking about you two for the next few days, I'm sure."

Edward said, "Since we are grateful for our guests, let's bow our heads for silent prayer."

A beef and vegetable soup was passed around the table, and as usual, a loaf of bread with jam. David and I were hungry from the long day, and the food was so good, as always.

Elizabeth had made a pizza with a cornbread crust. David does not like mushrooms, and I could tell that he saw them on the pizza, so he did not eat any. But I did, and it was delicious. It was also topped with their homemade sausage, onions, cheese and potatoes. He really missed out.

Christina and I reminisced about when I had taught Evangeline and Damaris how to paint in June.

"Damaris is very good for her age. She painted an overflowing bathtub!" I said.

As David and Edward continued their conversation about building our house, Edward gestured to two large triangle-shaped windows in the sunroom. He explained he had bought them at about half price because they had come from a house that was never completed. Doors, lights, and windows from the unfinished house were discounted and sold by the builder.

Edward recommended we look for people who sell used doors, lights, and windows when we build our house. David said he had heard of that from a friend of his who had done the same thing, but I had never heard of it before. I would certainly rather not pay full price for things for our house—as long as they are in fair condition.

Edward, Elizabeth, and Christina asked David all about his job and his family. When David mentioned his grandparents were Mennonite, they asked what kind of Mennonite they were and if they spoke any kind of German.

"I didn't realize there are several types of Mennonite," I said. "Are there New Order and Old Order, like the Amish?"

"Actually, there are also several branches of Amish under New Order and Old Order. New and Old Order are just two broad categories," Christina explained.

"Oh, I see. I had always thought the only two types were Old and New Order, but I guess that would be like categorizing Christians as either Catholic or Protestant."

"Yes! That is true!" Christina agreed, smiling.

"So, what type of Amish are you?" I asked Elizabeth.

"You could say we are Old Order," she said, but she did not go into much detail. I am not sure if they are a specific type of Old Order Amish or not. "Save some room for dessert—crumb cake and peaches!"

Of course, I should have known there would be an amazing dessert. There was always dessert. Christina put a plate of cut up crumb cake on the table with a bowl of homemade canned peaches. Everyone started taking a slice of cake and pouring milk on top of it, except David. He looked a little unsure of their customary way of eating dessert.

"This probably seems a little odd to you, but this is how we like to eat dessert. You don't have to try it if you don't want to," Elizabeth said to him when she realized he had skipped the milk.

"Well, why not?" he said and poured some milk on his cake. With the peaches on top it was delicious. I almost took a second slice, but I was already full and we started clearing the table.

"*Spiele* Candyland!" Damaris and Evangeline cried and pulled the Candyland board game off the shelf.

"Well, that's a game I know how to play," David said and started setting it up with them.

"David's family loves board games. We play a board game or card game almost every time I go over," I told them.

"My family has always played games, even when we were growing up," David commented.

"What kind of games do you play?" Edward asked David.

"Monopoly, chess, checkers, Life…"

"Oh, yes, I played chess growing up too," Edward said. He was familiar with several of the board games David mentioned. The Amish play many board games.

While Edward and David played with the girls, I did dishes with Christina and Elizabeth. I dried dishes while Elizabeth washed, and Christina put them away.

"Tell me about your family," Elizabeth said as she washed a cup.

"I have five siblings. My brother and his wife are expecting a baby right after our wedding. I also have two nieces."

"Ah, so you are from a big family. Do you have a job?"

"I actually just quit working at the salon where I was working and started working in my mom's salon in her house. One day I want to have my own salon in my house once it is built. Then I can have my own business in my home and still be able to write books and raise my own children when that time comes." I know the Amish do not encourage mothers to have jobs, but I think they respect the fact that David and I plan for me to work from home and are also considering homeschooling our future children.

When the last dish was put away, David looked at the clock which read 7:30 p.m. We had a two-hour drive ahead of us and still had to visit Caleb. So, we told them we had to leave. I asked Christina if I could come for a longer visit in the summer sometime, and we agreed that we would plan it later on. We thanked them graciously for dinner and the visit, then drove down the lane to Caleb's.

(Below is a photo of some buggies in Caleb's barn.)

Caleb's family had just finished dinner, and we sat down at the same couch where I had first met Caleb's family two years ago. Caleb lit a gas lamp on the wall which hurt my eyes to look at because of its intensity. Caleb and his wife, Rosie, pulled up a seat.

"We were in the area and decided to drop by," I explained.

"I received a message from you on my store phone saying you were lost earlier today. Did you have trouble for long?" Caleb asked.

"I left that message when we were very lost, but right after we found our way, and I forgot to call you back. I figured we would see you before you got the message anyway." I laughed. "Our GPS is usually very helpful, but ours led us in the totally wrong direction because we had the wrong address at first."

As the other two Amish couples had before them, Caleb and Rosie asked David about his job, and he also told them about his Mennonite family background. We told them about the land we are considering, and Caleb acknowledged that it was a fair price for a five-acre lot. It was right across the street from my parent's house.

Usually, when the Amish buy lots, they buy much bigger ones for their farms. Irvin and his wife own eighty acres! I grew up on fifty acres. We also told them about how my dad is a builder and is going to build our home for us, and then how we will buy it from him.

As I looked around the house, nothing was different than it had been two years ago when I had stayed here except for the cabinets, which had been only bare shelves when I had first arrived. "I see the cabinets are finished. They look really nice."

"Thank you. We finished them about a year and a half ago, but I guess that was after you were here," Caleb said.

The girls bustled around the kitchen, drying dishes from dinner and combing the younger girls' hair. They wove the hair into intricate braids which were held in place atop their heads by strips of yarn and small clips. One girl walked by with her hair down, which reached her knees. It was probably still drying from her shower. I marveled at its extreme length and recalled how as a child I had aspired to grow my hair that long, but had only grown it to my waist. I wondered how often hair that long would be caught on things, how hard it was to take care of or how tangled it became. Because they grew up with hair that long, they probably had taking care of it down to a science.

It was time to go. We thanked the family for letting us drop in and headed home. David was so glad he was able to meet my Amish friends that I have been writing about in this book, which he has read. He now has faces to go with the names and has seen the homes I described in this book.

He had loved talking with Edward and learning about the Amish ways and customs. I was so glad I was able to share with him something so dear to me. We drove home, reminiscing about the fun day and dreaming about our future together as I sang along with the radio and began writing this down.

Before this day, I had thought this story was complete, but I have realized it is an ongoing adventure. I look forward to the next time I visit Unity or Lancaster, which will hopefully be soon. (Update: we now go to Lancaster every Christmas for a week to visit family.)

Visiting an Amish Family in Lancaster, Pennsylvania

December 2014

Every year my husband David and I travel to Pennsylvania along with all our relatives to see his grandparents. Our relatives live all over the country from Maine to California but we all meet in Lancaster to celebrate Christmas together every year.

David's grandparents are Mennonite, and they know many of the Amish families in Lancaster because David's grandpa was one of their drivers. Whenever an Amish person has a trip to make that is too long or inconvenient for a horse and buggy, they often will hire a driver.

(Below are some photos of Amish farms we saw while driving through Lancaster County.)

(Below is a farm in Lancaster County.)

(Below is a photo of the farm my mother-in-law grew up on in Lancaster County. She was raised Mennonite.)

One Sunday after church we drove to an Amish home where a family had invited us to have dinner with them—all twenty-six of us.

(Below are photos of their farm.)

They lived on a lane off from the main road next to another farm that had sheep. One of the lambs had escaped the fence and was darting around, trying to get back into the fence.

(Above is an Amish barn near the Amish family's house.)

We parked in the driveway next to their buggy. I thought it was funny to see a buggy next to all of our cars!

I was so excited to meet an Amish family from Pennsylvania. Whenever I mention to people that I lived with the Amish to do research for my books, they always assume I went to Lancaster. I never knew any Amish from Lancaster until now.

We formed a line to meet the Amish couple and their six boys. Their names were Barbie and Ephraim, and we shook hands and went inside the second story of their barn.

(Below is a view from the barn window.)

It was a large room with tables, chairs, and a ping pong table. One table was set with a buffet of meats, cheese cubes, pretzels, veggies, and cookies. There was also a pot of hot cocoa on the propane stove and some punch.

Everyone sat down and started talking amongst each other, but I didn't want to miss a minute of what the Amish had to say. I hung around them, hovering, listening in on conversations. Then Grandpa spoke up. "Ashley writes Amish books."

Suddenly the room went quiet as the Amish couple looked at me. "What are your books about?"

The room stayed quiet as I awkwardly told them about the Amish community in Unity, Maine, and how I had stayed with three different families for a total of ten days. I told them that I used what I learned to write two Amish novels and a documentary of my time there.

Ephraim asked, "Are the Amish there different there than here in Lancaster?"

"I'm not sure yet because I don't know as much about the Amish in Pennsylvania. All the communities are different."

Barbie asked, "Will you write about this experience in your books?"

"I won't if you don't want me to, but I never use last names anyway."

"We don't mind at all," she said, and I assured her I wouldn't share any personal information like their address or last names.

Finally, people started talking again. My awkward feeling subsided. I really hate being the center of attention.

We ate lunch, and we couldn't get enough of the cubes of meat. I asked Barbie what they were made of, and she told me it was venison meat from a deer her neighbor shot. Growing up with my father being an experienced hunter, this didn't faze me at all.

"Do the Amish go hunting here?" I asked.

"Yes, but guns are strictly used for only hunting."

It is the same way for the Amish in Maine.

Barbie made some wonderful ginger cookies dipped in white chocolate which everyone raved about. I looked up a similar recipe online so I can make them sometime.

As we ate, some of our aunts and cousins asked me if the Amish boys were not allowed to talk to us. The six brothers ate on the opposite side of the room, eating and talking quietly among themselves.

"When I was in Unity, none of the Amish boys and young men spoke a word to me. I didn't know if they are not allowed to speak to young women who are not Amish, or if they were just shy or didn't know what to say. Maybe they didn't want to seem forward. I really don't know, but these boys do seem very shy."

However, after a while, some of our cousins walked over and asked the Amish boys in the corner to play a board game with them, and they did, so I guess they were just shy. However, the rules might be different in Unity. I had never had the courage to ask when I was there.

After lunch, the adults started talking with Barbie and Ephraim as the kids played ping pong and other games. I pulled up a chair to listen to what they were talking about. It was hard to hear—there were so many people in the room.

Ephraim told us, "We host church in this room once every ten months or so because the Amish here in Pennsylvania have church in Amish homes. When everyone sits on benches, we can fit two hundred fifty people in here."

I was shocked because twenty-six of us made it feel a little crowded.

"In Unity, they have a building that doubles as a church and a school. They also don't have refrigerators. They have rooms under their houses with huge blocks of ice to keep food cold," I told him.

Ephraim showed us a building in the distance that was where he had gone to school. Just like in Maine, they only go to school until the eighth grade.

"When I was young, there was a time when some Amish parents went to jail for not sending their children to school after the eighth grade." He went on to tell stories of parents he'd known who'd been arrested, which was shocking. "Now, it is accepted as part of our religion, so the children do not have to legally go to high school."

I asked to use the bathroom, and Barbie led me inside the house. There was a hanging battery-operated lantern/flashlight in the bathroom like I used in Unity.

(Below are photos of their kitchen.)

I wanted to see if anything was different from what they had in Unity. The first thing I noticed was that they had a refrigerator, as I mentioned earlier.

They had a massive kitchen, and on the counter were several boys' black hats that belonged to their sons. I couldn't resist trying one on and taking a picture on my phone.

They had a nice living room, and the home was uncluttered and minimally decorated. Only a few pictures and a calendar hung on the wall, and the pictures were not of people but of landscapes or animals. They do not let anyone take pictures of them, and they do not own pictures of others unless they are *Englishers*.

(Below is their living room.)

Several pairs of boys' black boots and shoes lined the wall near the door. I come from a family of five girls and one boy. Six boys must be so different than what I grew up with!

I figured I better get back, so I returned to the barn, but not before snapping some quick pictures of the yard. They had a lovely little garden, which of course was almost frozen over, and rolling hills with a tree line that marked off the edge of their property. They had dozens of chickens and some goats.

I went back inside, and most of the family left to go back to where we were staying for the week, but I wanted to stay and talk more. Finally, now that most of the family had left, I could hear all of what was being said.

Ephraim said, "Our bishop travels from church to church. Each bishop is in charge of one or two churches."

"Unity didn't even have a bishop when I went. Instead, they had a few men who took turns speaking, since they were not close to other Amish communities and they were a small community. Maybe by now, since they have grown, they might have a bishop," I replied.

As we were cleaning, I asked Barbie, "Do you know if the Amish would ever adopt a child?"

"I don't know anyone who has, but certainly an Amish family might adopt a child, especially if they can't have children of their own."

"I was wondering because in one of my novels, an Amish family adopts a baby girl."

"I just don't know what the legal process would be or if an Amish family would use a lawyer."

She left to play a game of Apples to Apples with some of the kids. Ephraim told me about how he fixes farm machinery for work, and a few of his sons were done with school and apprenticing with him.

Our grandpa used to work for that company when he was driving for Amish families.

We stayed for another hour or so, talking. Ephraim asked me more questions about my stay with the Amish, and Barbie came back over and said she would love to learn about the Amish in Maine and see how they do some things differently.

"I'll mail you a copy as a thank you gift for having us over for lunch!" I promised, and they wrote their address down for me on a napkin. Now I could even write them letters if I wanted to. I am mailing out the book to them this week.

Sadly, we had to leave. I loved learning about the Amish in Lancaster, Pennsylvania and asking them all my questions. My husband could easily see my fascination and enjoyment.

"You were really in your element!" he commented later that day. I was so glad to have met an Amish family in Lancaster. It was one more fascinating learning experience that I will use to write my Amish novels.

Not only do I look forward to visiting the Amish again with David, but I look forward to our lives together as a married couple and discovering everything together. Just like life, this ongoing true story of our adventures together will be unpredictable, and there are so many future stories that have not yet been written that I can't wait to experience. Be watching for more of my adventures!

Update: January 6th, 2020

I owe so much to my Amish friends. If it wasn't for them, I wouldn't have had the knowledge and hands-on experiences that I used to write my Amish series. I now make a full-time income self-publishing my Amish novels, and I am starting my second Amish series this year, The Amish Fairytale Series.

This career allows me to stay home with my children, be with them every day, and home school them while doing work I love. It's given me so much more than I ever wanted.

My book sales have wildly increased in 2019 with the release of *Amish Amnesia*, doubling my sales in 2018. I plan on doubling them again in 2020.

I have big plans to release several more Amish novels in my Covert Police Detectives Series in 2020 and 2021 including *Amish Alias, Amish Assassin,* and *Amish Identity*. For my new Amish Fairytale Series, I am working on *Amish Beauty and the Beast, Princess and the Amish Pauper,* and I have plans for an *Amish Aladdin, Sleeping Beauty*, and *Amish Cinderella*.

All my life I dreamed of becoming a novelist. I'm amazed every day I'm living my dream life, and I'm so grateful to God and my Amish friends for making it possible.

In December 2019 we (me, my husband, and our three children) visited Lancaster County for Christmas to visit relatives, as we do every year. This year, I decided to go to an Amish tourist attraction, which was a first for me. I went to Aaron and Jessica's buggy rides, which I highly recommend.

When I told the driver, an elderly Amish man, that I write Amish books for a living he quizzed me the entire time.

"You write Amish books?" he asked, surprised. "Well, then tell us what you know about the Amish." The Amish buggy—which was actually called a wagon—was quite large and was filled with about ten people.

Usually people ask them questions but instead he asked me to tell him what I knew about the Amish and he said he enjoyed it being the other way around.

As we drove along on the half-hour ride, we passed many Amish farms and businesses, and the driver told us all about them.

But throughout the ride he asked me many questions about my books, and I asked him some things I'd been wanting to know too. I asked him if it was a myth that Amish don't wear buttons, and he said twenty years ago they did not wear buttons, but now they do. He also told me the TV show Amish Mafia is fake and all paid actors (which I knew) and that he even knew many of the actors who had been on the show, who even admitted how fake it was. In fact, I interviewed one of them, who also told me the show was fake and not accurate, which is why he quit the show. Go to my website www.ashleyemmaauthor.com to get my free ex-Amish interviews.

I also asked him if he knew any Amish who had adopted a child, because that is in one of my novels, and he said yes, he knew of several Amish families who had adopted.

When the ride ended, he shook my hand and said he really enjoyed talking with me. I wish I could have gotten a photo with him, but I knew it's against their beliefs, so I didn't ask.

However, these are the photos I took near that area that day.

(Above: The horse was licking my hand, so that's why I was laughing.)

(Above: An Amish buggy in the local Wal Mart parking lot.)

AMISH COUNTRY HOMESTEAD

The first replica Old Order Amish Home from which interpretive tours were conducted depicts the home life of a present day Amish family. Together with the Amish Experience Theater and Amish Country Farmlands Tours, the Homestead represents our best efforts at explaining the rich cultural heritage and traditions, both past and present, of our Amish neighbors.

- Built 1959 -

(Above: The Amish Experience is next door to Aaron and Jessica's Buggy Rides.)

(Above: There is something so serene and beautiful about seeing Amish clothing hanging out on a clothesline on a sunny day.)

Thank you for joining me on my Amish adventures!

Praise for *Undercover Amish*

"*Undercover Amish* is the first Amish novel I've read, and I have to say it was a fascinating and insightful look into a different culture. Ashley Emma clearly did extensive research on the subject and portrayed this group in a compassionate, thoughtful manner. Couple her careful handling of this society with her compelling characters and heart-racing plot, and you've got a real winner!"

--Staci Troilo, author of **Mind Control, Bleeding Heart** and many other titles

"What can I say, I LOVE mysteries! I love getting to know the characters, their motivations and then trying to figure out the outcomes. I am therefore delighted to have discovered *Undercover Amish*. Not only does the main character, Olivia, has a unique background of being Amish, but the trajectory of her life from that background to becoming a policewoman is fascinating and totally unexpected. Not only did I find myself engrossed in the unraveling of a crime, but also in the learning about a culture, within my own country, about which I was, admittedly, basically ignorant. Kudos to Ashley Emma for creating this wonderful series. I can't wait to read more of them!"

--Leslie K. Malin, LCSW, psychotherapist, iLife Transition Coach, and author of **Cracked Open: Reflections on the Transformative Power of Failure, Fear, & Doubt** website/blog: http://www.JustThinkn.com

"*Undercover Amish* is a suspenseful, realistic work of fiction. Ashley weaves two opposite worlds together in a fast-paced story following

Detective Olivia Mast. Olivia's journey forces her to face issues of identity, rise up to work challenges, and eventually she finds love. It's an easy read that will keep you guessing until the end."

--J.P. Sterling, author of *Ruby in the Water*

"Buy this book! It's a five-star read in my opinion. Whether you have ever read Amish detective stories before or not, I know you'll like this one and be totally engaged from start to finish. The characters are well-developed, unique, quirky, and three-dimensional. I enjoyed the author giving her readers an inside view of the Amish community, especially during dangerous and unpredictable times. I eagerly await the sequel to this novel!"

--Wendy Pearson, moderator of **The Write Practice**

"I love a good mystery and this one has an interesting storyline. A relatively short read and kept me engaged and trying to guess the next twist. This is the kind of book I love to have when traveling or for an afternoon at the beach."

--C.L. Ferrari, bestselling author of *Enriching Your Retirement*

"Ashley Emma has crafted an intriguing crime mystery with a surprising twist. I didn't see that ending coming at all. And I'm a little jealous. Once I got into this book, I couldn't put it down."

-Michael Wilkinson, bestselling author of *A Father's Guide to Raising Daughters*

"I really enjoyed this book, right through the last page!! Undercover Amish is a compelling read that will keep you going until the very end! The only disappointing thing for me about Undercover Amish was when the story ended—I already miss the main characters!"

--Sue M Wilson, author of **Home Matters**

www.suemwilson.com

"This book will take no time at all to grab you and take you into a world most of us know nothing about. Because the author spent time with the Amish, Ashley Emma is able to present her story in a truthful manner. After you read this, you will feel as though you know enough to say you understand them. (You may even find yourself wanting to wear more solid colors.) But murder has crept into their safe haven. Olivia, the main character, who was once Amish comes back and investigates a string of crimes, all while being undercover. I highly recommend this book. Ashley keeps you on the edge of your horse and buggy seat while making you fall in love with her characters. You'll be sorry once it is over. Thankfully there are more of her books to read coming soon!"

--Emily L. Pittsford, author of A Most Incredible Witness

Want to learn more? Here are my recommended books and movies about the Amish:

A History of the Amish by Steven M. Nolt

20 Most Asked Questions About the Amish and Mennonites, by Merle Good and Phyllis Pellman Good (This was the book I studied before going to Unity and it really helped me.)

Fields of Corn: The Amish of Lancaster County by Sarah Price

When the Heart Cries
When the Morning Comes
When the Soul Mends
Hope of Refuge
Bridge of Peace
by Cindy Woodsmall
(These were the first Amish novels I read.)

Movies:
Amish Grace
Saving Sarah Cain
Plain Truth
The Shunning

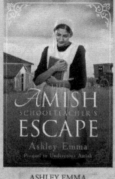
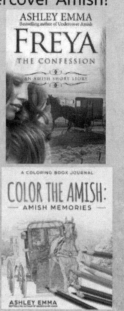

Other books by Ashley Emma on Amazon

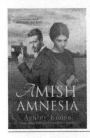 

Coming soon:

Check out my author Facebook page to see rare photos from when I lived with the Amish in Unity, Maine.

Click here to join my free Facebook group The Amish Book Club where I share free Amish books weekly!

Sample chapter of Amish Alias by Ashley Emma

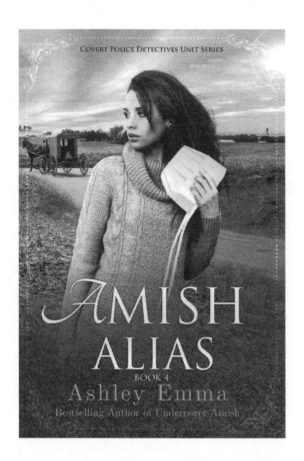

Chapter One

"Mom, are we there yet?" nine-year-old Charlotte Cooper

asked from the back seat of her parents' van. Her legs pumped

up and down in anticipation. Mom had said they were going to a

farm where her aunt lived, and she couldn't wait to see the

animals. The ride was taking forever.

"Just a few more minutes, honey," Mom said from the driver's seat.

Charlotte put her coloring book down and patted the lollipop in her pocket Mommy had given her for the trip. She was tempted to eat it now but decided to save it for the ride home. She hoped it wouldn't melt in her pocket. The van was hot even though she was wearing shorts and her favorite pink princess T-shirt. Charlotte shoved her damp blonde curls out of her eyes.

The van passed a yellow diamond-shaped sign that had a black silhouette of a horse and carriage on it. "Mommy, what does that sign mean?"

"It's a warning to drive slowly because there are horses and buggies on the road here."

"*What?* Horses and bugs?"

"No." Mom smiled. "They're called buggies. They're like the carriages you've seen in your storybooks. Except they are not pumpkin-shaped. They are black and shaped more like a box."

Charlotte imagined a black box being pulled by a horse. If she were a princess, she would like a pumpkin carriage much better. "Why are there buggies here?"

"The folks who live in this area don't drive cars."

They don't drive cars? Charlotte thought. "Then what do they drive?"

"They only drive buggies," Mom said.

How fast do buggies go? Charlotte wondered. *Not fast as a car, I bet.* "Why would anyone not drive a car? They're so much faster than buggies."

"I know, honey. Some people are just …different." Mom glanced at Charlotte in the rear-view mirror. "But being different isn't a bad thing."

Charlotte gazed out the window. Even though they had just passed a pizza place a few minutes ago, all she could see now were huge fields and plain-looking houses.

There was nothing around. This looked like a boring place to live. What did people do to have fun here besides play outside?

A horse and carriage rumbled past them on the unpaved road going in the other direction. A girl wearing a blue dress and a white bonnet sat on the top seat, guiding a dark brown horse. She looked just like a picture Charlotte had seen in her history book at school. "Look, Mom." Charlotte pointed at the big black box on wheels.

"It's not polite to point, Charlie."

Charlotte dropped her hand to her side. "Why is that girl dressed like a pilgrim, Mom? She's wearing a bonnet. Are we near Plymouth Plantation?"

Mom didn't answer. Maybe she was too distracted. She seemed really focused on the mailbox up ahead.

"We're here," Mom said and turned onto a long driveway.

Charlotte gaped at the chocolate-colored horses in the fields and the clucking chickens congregating in the front yard. The van bounced over bumps on the gravel path leading to a huge tan house with bright blue curtains hanging in the windows. The dark red roof had a large metal pipe coming out of the top with smoke coming out of it, and behind the house stood a big red barn. Charlotte wondered how many animals were in there.

Mom parked the van and helped Charlotte out. "I'm going inside to talk to your Aunt Esther. I don't want to bring you inside because... Well... You should just wait here. I won't be long."

"Can I walk around?"

Before Mom could answer, a young boy about Charlotte's age walked out of the barn. He saw them and waved.

"Can I go play with him?" Charlotte asked.

"Hi!" The boy ran over. "I've never seen you around here before. Want to go see the animals in the barn?"

"Can I go in the barn with him?" Charlotte asked her mother.

"What's your name?" Mom asked the boy. "Is Esther your *Maam*?"

"I'm Elijah. No, she's not my mother. My *Maam* and *Daed* are out running errands, so I'm playing here until they get back. My parents are best friends with Esther and Irvin. I come here all the time. I know my way around the barn real well."

Mom crossed her arms and bit her lip, then looked at Charlotte. "I suppose you can go in. But stay away from the horses."

"We will, ma'am," said Elijah.

Charlotte and Elijah took off running toward the barn. They ran into the dim interior and she breathed in. It smelled like hay and animals, just like the county fair she had gone to last fall with her mom and dad. To the left, she heard pigs squealing. To the right, she heard sheep bleating.

Which animals should we go see first? Charlotte wondered, tapping her toes on the hay-covered floor.

Elijah leaned over the edge of the sheep pen, patting a lamb's nose. He was dressed in plain black and white clothing and a straw hat. His brown hair reached the collar of his white shirt. He even wore suspenders. Charlotte glanced down at her princess T-shirt and wondered why he didn't dress like other kids at her school. Every kid she knew wore cool T-shirts. *Why are the people here dressed in such plain, old-fashioned clothes?*

Charlotte stepped forward. He turned around, looked at her, and grinned. "So what's your name, anyway?"

"I'm Charlotte. Well, you can call me Charlie."

"Charlie? That's a boy's name."

"It's my nickname. I like it."

"Suit yourself. Where you from?"

"Portland, Maine. Where are you from?"

"I live in Smyrna."

"Oh." Charlotte raised an eyebrow. Smyrna? Where was

that?

Elijah smiled. "It's a bigger Amish community in northern Maine."

Charlotte shrugged. "Never heard of it."

Elijah shrugged. "Want to pet the sheep?"

"Yeah." They climbed up onto some boards stacked along the edge of the enclosure. Several of the animals sniffed their fingers and let out high-pitched noises. "They sound like people," Charlotte said. "The lambs sound like babies crying, and the big sheep sound like adults making sheep noises."

They laughed at that, and when the biggest sheep looked at them and cried *baaa* loudly, they laughed even harder.

Charlotte looked at the boy next to her, who was still watching the sheep. A small smear of dirt covered some of the freckles on his cheek, and his brown eyes sparkled when he laughed. The hands that gripped the wooden boards of the sheep pen looked strong. She wondered what it would be like if he held her hand. As she watched Elijah tenderly stroke the nose of a sheep, she smiled.

When one lamb made an especially loud, funny noise that

sounded like a baby crying, Elijah threw his head back as he laughed, and his hat fell off. Charlotte snatched it up and turned it over in her hands. "Wow. I've never held a straw hat before. We don't have these where I live. I thought people only wore ones like these in the olden days."

Elijah shrugged. "What's wrong with that?"

"Nothing." Charlotte smiled shyly and offered it back to him. "Here you go."

Elijah held up his hand. "You can keep it if you want." He smiled at her with those dark eyes.

Charlotte got a funny feeling in her stomach. It was the same way she felt just before saying her lines on stage in the school play. She knew she should say, "Thank you," like Mom had taught her. But she couldn't speak the words. Instead, she took the lollipop out of her pocket and handed it to him.

"Thanks," Elijah said, eyes wide.

"You're welcome."

Elijah gestured to Charlie's ankle. "Hey, what happened to your ankle?"

Charlie looked down at the familiar sight of the zig-zagging surgical scars that marred her ankle. "I've had a lot of surgeries on my ankle. When I was born it wasn't formed right, but now it's all better and I can run and jump like other kids."

"Does it hurt?"

"No, not anymore. But it hurt when I had the surgeries. I had, like, six surgeries."

"Wow, really?"

"Charlotte!" Mom called. "We have to leave. Right now."

"Thanks for the hat, Elijah." Charlotte turned to leave. Then she stopped, turned around, and kissed him on the cheek.

Embarrassment flushed Elijah's cheeks.

Uh oh. Her own face heated, Charlotte sprinted toward her mother's voice.

"Get in the car," Mom said. "Your aunt refused to speak with us. She wants us to leave."

Charlotte had never heard her mother sound so upset. She climbed into the van, and Mom hastily buckled her in.

"Why didn't she want to talk to us, Mom?" Charlotte said.

Mom sniffed and shook her head. "It's hard to explain, baby."

"Why are you crying, Mom?"

"I just wanted to talk to my sister. And she wanted us to go away."

"That's not very nice," Charlotte said.

"I know, Charlie. Some people aren't nice. Remember that."

The van sped down the driveway as Charlotte clutched the straw hat.

"Why are you going so fast?" Charlotte said and craned her neck, hoping to see Elijah. She saw him standing outside the barn with one hand holding the lollipop and the other hand on his cheek where she'd kissed him. He was smiling crookedly.

Mom looked in the rearview mirror at Charlotte.

"Sorry," Mom said and slowed down.

Charlotte settled in her seat. She hoped she'd see Elijah again, and maybe he'd be her very own prince charming like in her fairytale books.

But Mom never took her to the farm again.

Chapter Two

Fifteen years later

"Hi, Mom," twenty-four-year-old Charlie said, stepping into her mother's hospital room in the cancer ward. "I brought you Queen Anne's lace, your favorite." She set the vase of white flowers on her mom's bedside table.

"Oh, thank you, honey." Mom smiled, but her face looked thin and pale, a bright scarf covering her head. "Come sit with me." She patted the edge of the bed, and Charlie sat down, taking her mother's frail hand.

"You know why Queen Anne's lace are my favorite flowers?" Mom asked quietly.

Charlie shook her head.

"Growing up in the Amish community, we'd get tons of Queen Anne's lace in the fields every summer. My sister, Esther, and I would try to pick as much as we could before the grass was cut down for hay. At the end of every August, we'd also check all around for milkweed and look for monarch caterpillars before they were destroyed. We'd try to save as many of them as we could. We'd put them in jars and watch them make their chrysalises, then watch in amazement as they transformed into butterflies and escaped them. I used to promise myself that I'd get out into the world one day, just like the butterflies, and leave the Amish community behind. I knew it would be painful to leave everyone and everything I knew, but it would be worth it."

"And was it?" Charlie asked, leaning in close.

"Of course. It was both—painful and worth it. I don't regret leaving though. I never have. I miss my family, and I wish I could talk to them, but it was their choice to shun me. Not mine." Determination still shone in Mom's tired eyes. "I had already been baptized into the church when I left. That's why I was shunned. I still don't understand that rule. I still don't understand so many of their rules. I couldn't bear a life without music, and the Amish aren't allowed to play instruments. I wanted to go to college, but that's forbidden, too. Then there was your father, the Englisher, the outsider. It was too much for them, even for Esther. She swore she would never shun me. In the end, she turned her back on me, too."

Mom stared at the Queen Anne's lace, as if memories of her childhood were coming back to her. She wiped away a tear.

"And that's why she turned you away that day you took me to see her," Charlie concluded.

"Yes. Honestly, I've been so hurt, but I'm not angry with her. I don't want to hold a grudge. I can't decide if we should try to contact her or not to tell her I'm..." Mom's voice trailed off, and she blew out a lungful of air. She shook her head and looked down. "She wouldn't come to see me, anyway. There's no point."

"Really? Your own sister wouldn't come to see you, even under these circumstances?" Charlie gasped.

"I doubt it. She'd risk being shunned if she did." Mom patted Charlie's hand. "Don't get me wrong. I loved growing up Amish. There are so many wonderful things about it. They help each other in hard times, and they're the most tightly knit group of people I've ever met. Their faith is rock solid, most of the time. But most people only see their quaint, simple lifestyle and don't realize the Amish are human, too. They make mistakes just like the rest of us. Sometimes they gossip or say harsh things."

"Of course. Everyone does that," Charlie said.

Mom continued. "And they have such strict rules. Rules that were too confining for me. Once your father taught me how to play the piano at the old museum, I couldn't understand why they wouldn't allow such a beautiful instrument that can even be used to worship the Lord."

Mom shook her head. "I just had to leave. But I will always miss my family. I'll miss how God and family always came first, how it was their priority. Life was simpler, and people were close. We worked hard, but we had a lot of fun." Mom's face lit up. "We'd play so many games outside, and even all kinds of board games inside. Even work events were fun. And the food… Don't get me started on the delicious food. Pies, cakes, casseroles, homemade bread… I spent countless hours cooking and baking with my mother and sisters. There are many things I've missed. But I'm so glad I left because I married your father and had my two beautiful daughters. I wouldn't trade you two for anything. I wouldn't ever go back and do it differently."

Gratitude swelled in Charlie's chest, and she swallowed a lump in her throat. "But how could Aunt Esther do that to you? I just don't understand."

Mom shrugged her frail shoulders, and the hospital gown rustled with the movement. "She didn't want to end up like me—shunned. I don't blame her. It's not her fault, really. It's all their strict rules. I don't think God would want us to cut off friends and family when they do something wrong. And I didn't even do anything wrong by leaving. I'll never see it their way." Mom hiked her chin in defiance.

What had her mother been like at Charlie's age? Charlie smiled, imagining Mom as a determined, confident young woman. "Well, your community shouldn't have done that to you, Mom. Especially Aunt Esther, your own sister."

"I don't want that to paint you a negative picture of the Amish. They really are wonderful people, and it's beautiful there. You probably would have loved growing up there."

Charlie shook her head with so much emphasis that loose tendrils of hair fell from her ponytail. "No. I'm glad we live here. I wouldn't have liked those rules either. I'm glad you left, Mom. You made the right choice."

*

Elijah Hochstettler trudged into his small house after a long day of work in the community store with Irvin. He pulled off his boots, loosened his suspenders, and started washing his hands, getting ready to go to dinner at the Holts' house. He splashed water on his beardless face, the trademark of a single Amish man, thinking of his married friends who all had beards. Sometimes he felt like he was the last single man in the entire community.

He sat on his small bed with a sigh and looked around his tiny home. From this spot, he could see almost the entire structure. The community had built this house for him when he'd moved here when he was eighteen, just after his family had died. The Holts had been looking out for him ever since.

His dining room and living room were one room, and the bathroom was in the corner. It was a small cabin, but he was grateful that Irvin and the other men in the community had helped him build it. Someday he wanted to build a real house, if he ever found a woman to settle down with.

Another night alone. He wished he had a wife. He was only in his early twenties, but he had dreamed of getting married ever since he was a young teenager. He knew a wife was a gift from God, and he had watched how much in love his parents had been growing up. He could hardly wait to have such a special bond with one person.

If only his parents were still alive. Even if Elijah did have children one day, they would only have one set of grandparents. How Elijah's parents would have loved to have grandchildren. At least he had Esther and Irvin Holt. They were almost like parents to him. But even with the Holts right next door, he still felt lonely sometimes.

"At least I have You, Lord," Elijah said quietly.

He opened his Bible to see his familiar bookmark. His fingers brushed the waxy paper of the lollipop wrapper he had saved from his childhood. He had eaten the little orange sucker right away, since it was such a rare treat. But even after all these years, he could still not part with the simple wrapper.

Maybe it was silly. Over a decade had passed since that blonde *Englisher* girl had given it to him. How long had it been? Twelve years? Fifteen years? Her name was Charlie, short for Charlotte. He knew he'd never forget it because it was such an odd nickname for a girl. He remembered her laughing eyes. And the strange, exciting feeling she had given him.

Over the years, Elijah had been interested in a few girls. But he'd never pursued any of them because he didn't feel God calling him to. He never felt the kind of connection with them that he'd experienced with that girl in the barn when he was ten years old. He longed to feel that way about a woman. Maybe it had just been feelings one only had during childhood, but whatever it was, it had felt so genuine.

All this time, he'd kept the wrapper as a reminder to pray for that girl. For over fifteen years, he'd asked God to bring Charlie back into his life.

As he turned the wrapper over in his calloused hands, he prayed, "Lord, please keep her safe, help her love you more every day, and help me also love you more than anything. And if you do bring her back to me, please help me not mess it up."

He set down his Bible and walked to the Holts' house for supper.

The aroma of beef stew warmed his insides as he stepped into the familiar kitchen. Esther was slicing her homemade bread at the table.

"Hello, Elijah."

"Hi, Esther. I was wondering, do you remember that young girl named Charlie and her mother who came here about fifteen years ago? She was blonde, and she and her mother were *Englishers.* Who were they?"

"I don't know what you're talking about." Esther cut into the bread with more force than necessary.

"It's hard to forget. Her mom was so upset when they left. In fact, she said you refused to speak to them and made them leave. What was that all about?" He knew he was prying, but the words had just tumbled out. He couldn't stop them. "And I remember her name was Charlie because it's such an odd name for a girl."

"It was no one, Elijah. It does not concern you," she said stiffly.

"What happened? Something must have happened for you to not want to talk to her. Will they come back?" he pressed, knowing he should stop talking, but he couldn't. "It's not like you at all to turn someone away at the door."

"It's a long story, one I don't care to revisit. I do not suspect they will ever come back. Now, do not ask me again," she said in such a firm voice that he jumped in surprise. Esther had always been a mild and sweet woman. What had made her so angry? Elijah had never seen her act like that before.

Elijah knew he was crossing the line by a mile, but he just had to know who the girl was. "Esther, please, I just want to know—"

Esther lifted her head slowly, looking him right in the eye, and set her knife down on the table with a thud.

"Elijah," she said in a pained, low voice. Her eyes narrowed, giving her an expression that was so unlike her usual smiling face. "The woman was my sister. I can't talk about what happened. I just can't. It's more complicated and terrible than you'll ever know. Don't ask me about her again."

*

The following night, Dad got a phone call from the hospital while they were having dinner at home. Since Dad was sitting close enough to her, Charlie overheard the voice on the phone.

"Come to the hospital now. I'm afraid this could possibly be Joanna's last night," the woman on the phone told them.

"What's going on?" Zoe, Charlie's eight-year-old sister asked, looking between Charlie and their father. "Dad? Charlie?"

Dad just hung his head.

Charlie's eyes stung with tears as she patted her younger sister's hand. "We have to leave right now, Zoe. We have to go see Mom."

As Dad sped them to the hospital, Charlie said, "Dad, if you're going to drive like this, you really should wear your seat belt. I mean, you always should, but especially right now."

"You know I hate seat belts. There shouldn't even be a law that we have to wear them. It should be our own choice. And I hate how constricting they are. Besides, that's the last thing on my mind right

232

now. Let's not have this argument again tonight."

Charlie sighed. How many times had they argued about seat belts over the years? Even Mom had tried to get Dad to wear one, but he wouldn't budge.

They arrived at the hospital and rushed to Mom's room.

It all felt unreal as they entered the white room containing her frail mother. Charlie halted at the door.

She couldn't do this.

She felt her throat constrict, and for a moment her stomach felt sick. "No, Dad, I can't," she whispered, her hand on her stomach. "I can't say goodbye."

"Charlie, this is your last chance. If you don't, you'll regret it forever. I know you can do it. You are made of the same stuff as your mother," he said and pulled her close, stroking her hair.

Compliments were rare from her father, but she was too heartbroken to truly appreciate it.

He let out a sob, and Charlie's heart wrenched. She hated it when her dad cried, which Charlie had only seen once or twice in her life. Zoe came over and wrapped her arms around them, then they walked over to the bed together.

They held her hand and whispered comforting words. They cried and laughed a little at fond memories. Her father said his goodbyes, Zoe said her goodbyes, and then it was Charlie's turn.

She did not bother trying to stop the flow of her tears. Sorrow crushed her spirit, and no matter how hard she tried she could not see how any silver lining could come from this. Was God punishing her for something? Why was He taking her beautiful, wonderful mother?

"Charlie, I love you," her mother whispered and clutched her hand with little strength.

"I love you too, Mom," Charlie choked out.

"Please promise me, Charlie. Chase your dreams and become a teacher."

"Okay, Mom. I will."

"I just want you to be happy."

"Mom, I will be. I promise."

"Take care of them."

"I will, Mom." She barely got the words out before another round of tears came.

"Thank you. I'll be watching."

Charlie nodded, unable to speak, biting her lip to keep from crying out.

"One more thing. There's something I need to tell you. Please tell your Aunt Esther that I forgive her. Promise me you will. And tell her I'm sorry. I am so sorry." Mom sobbed, and Charlie saw the same pain in her eyes she'd seen all those years ago after they left the Amish farm.

"Why, Mom? Sorry for what?"

"I lied to you yesterday, Charlie, when I said I wasn't angry with her. I didn't want you to think I was a bitter person. Honestly, I have been angry at her for years for shunning me. It was so hard to talk about. I'm so sorry I didn't tell you the whole story."

"It's okay, Mom. I love you."

"I love you too. Tell Esther I love her and that I'm sorry. I forgive her. I hope she forgives me too..." Regret shone in Mom's eyes, then her eyes fluttered closed and the monitor next to her started beeping loudly.

"Forgive you for what? Why does she need to forgive you?" Charlie asked, panic rising in her voice as her eyes darted to the monitor. "What's wrong? What's happening?"

"Her heart rate is dropping," the nurse said and called the doctor into the room.

Charlie's heart wrenched at the sight of Zoe weeping, begging Mom not to die. Dad reached for Mom.

"Mom!" Zoe screamed.

"I'm sorry," the nurse said to Dad. "This could be it."

The doctor assessed her and slowly shook his head, frowning. "I'm so sorry. We tried everything we could. There's nothing more we can do. We will give you some privacy. Please call us if you need anything. We are right down the hall."

Charlie stood on shaky legs, feeling like they would give out at any moment. The doctor continued talking, but his words sounded like muffled gibberish in her ears. He turned and walked out of the room.

Charlie squeezed Mom's hand. "Mom? Mom? Please, tell me what you want Aunt Esther to forgive you for." It seemed so important to Mom, and Charlie wasn't sure if Dad would talk about it, so this could be her last chance to find out. If Mom's dying wish was to ask Aunt Esther's forgiveness for something, Charlie wanted to honor it.

Mom barely opened her eyes and mumbled something incoherent.

"Joanna, we are all here." Dad took Mom's other hand, and Zoe stood by Mom's bed.

Then Mom managed to whisper, "I...love...you...all." Her eyes opened for one fleeting moment, and she looked at each of them. She gave a small smile. "I'm going with Jesus." Her eyes closed.

The machine beside them made one long beeping sound.

She was gone.

Zoe cried out. They held each other as they wept.

Charlie's heart felt literally broken. She sucked in some air, feeling her chest ache, as if there was no air left to breathe.

When they finally left the hospital, she was in a haze as her feet moved on auto pilot. After they got to the apartment, hours passed before they finished drying their tears.

What would Mom say to make her feel better? That this was God's will? Charlie knew that was exactly what she'd say.

Why did God *want* this to happen?

Why didn't He take me instead? Mom was so...good, she thought glumly.

Her whole life she had been taught about the perfect love of Jesus and His wonderful plan for her life. Why was this part of His plan? This was not a wonderful plan.

She fell on her bed, put her head down on her pillow and sighed. "God...please just help me get through this. I don't know what to think right now. Please help me stop doubting you and just trust You."

Someone knocked on the apartment door. When neither her father nor Zoe got up to see who it was, Charlie dragged herself off her bed and went to the door, opening it.

"Alex!" she cried in surprise.

Her ex-fiancé stood in the doorway in his crisp police uniform. Dad and Zoe quickly came over to see what was going on.

"I need to talk to you, Charlie," he told her with determination. He glanced at Charlie's dad and sister. "Alone."

"Not going to happen, Alex," Dad said, stomping towards Alex. "In fact, you broke my daughter's heart. You cheated on her. If she doesn't want to talk to you, she doesn't have to."

"This is terrible timing, Alex. My mother just passed away," Charlie told him, tears constricting her voice. "You should go."

"I'm really sorry. But I've got to tell you something important, Charlie," Alex insisted, taking hold of Charlie's arm a little too roughly. "Come talk to me in the hallway for one minute."

"No." Charlie shoved him away.

"Charlie!" Alex yelled and pulled on her arm again, harder this time. "Come on. I wouldn't be here if it wasn't really important."

"Enough. Get out of here right now, Alex. And don't come back, you hear?" Dad's tall, daunting form seemed to take up the entire doorway. He loomed over Alex threateningly.

The police officer backed away with his hands up and stormed down the stairs.

Charlie let out a sigh of relief. He was gone. For now.

If you enjoyed this sample, check out Amish Alias here on Amazon: https://www.amazon.com/Amish-Alias-Romantic-Suspense-Detectives-ebook/dp/B07ZCJBWJL/

Made in the USA
Columbia, SC
08 December 2021

50709723R00148